THE LAND OF CIGAM

THE LAND OF CIGAM

G. F. Kelton

To Doug

Merry Christmas

2007

Corky

G. F. Kelton

iUniverse, Inc.

New York Lincoln Shanghai

THE LAND OF CIGAM

iUniverse books may be ordered through booksellers or by contacting:

iUniverse
2021 Pine Lake Road, Suite 100
Lincoln, NE 68512
www.iuniverse.com
1-800-Authors (1-800-288-4677)

Because of the dynamic nature of the Internet, any Web addresses or links contained in this book may have changed since publication and may no longer be valid.

This is a work of fiction. All of the characters, names, incidents, organizations, and dialogue in this novel are either the products of the author's imagination or are used fictitiously.

ISBN: 978-0-595-46947-5 (pbk)
ISBN: 978-0-595-91231-5 (ebk)

Printed in the United States of America

To my daughter and son

Tracey and Jason

and all those who have helped and supported along the way.

PEOPLE OFTEN WONDER—

IS MAGIC REALLY THERE?

BUT IF YOU LOOK AND LISTEN CLOSELY,

MAGIC IS EVERYWHERE.

NOW I'M GOING TO SPIN A TALE,

LIKE THE WEB THAT THE SPIDER WEAVES.

AND WHEN I'M DONE, YOU'LL BE ONE

THAT UNDERSTANDS AND BELIEVES.

The Story Begins

It was early morning as a shadowy figure entered the Great Room of the castle. The figure approached an alter that stood at the far end of the Great Room. Resting in the Alter was a rock that glowed dimly in the early morning light.

With the wave of an arm, a hawk flew through a partially open window and landed on the edge of the Alter. The shadowy figure was that of a woman, who only a short time earlier was incredibly beautiful. As the moments passed by, her features became more and more hideous. An evil smile crossed her lips and with a rasping voice said, "Pargon, my beautiful, beautiful bird." She reached out and stroked Pargon's feathers.

"We have waited long and patiently for this moment and now the time has finally come."

The woman reached down into the Alter and picked up the rock, holding it in the palm of her hand. The soft light of the rock began to flicker as if the rock was afraid. The woman laughed softly as she stared at the rock, and then turned to Pargon.

"Pargon, I now possess enough power to open a portal into another dimension, but only for a short time. You will carry the rock and drop it into a deep watery grave where it will never again see the light of day. Do you understand?"

Pargon nodded his head.

"Good," smiled the woman. "When you return I will have a special treat for you, now go."

Pargon grabbed the rock with its talons and flew back out the window. As the hawk flew away, dark ominous clouds began to form over the castle and surrounding area.

The transformation in the woman was now complete. Her features now mirrored the evil that was within her, hideous and grotesque.

"When they awake," she whispered, "they will all be changed. I will drive them from the castle and my loyal subjects will hunt them down for sport, one by one until only the King is left. Then, I will deal with him myself."

Pargon flew through the portal and into a raging thunderstorm. The hawk could see a large body of water just ahead. The strong winds and rain made flying very difficult. As Pargon started over the water, a flash of lightning shattered the air nearby—almost hitting him. Pargon, stunned for a moment, dropped the rock. The rock fell into the water not far from shore. He circled the area several times while being battered by wind and rain. Certainly it was far enough from shore to accomplish the purpose and besides, he couldn't swim to get it. If he didn't leave soon, the portal would close. Pargon left, confident he had done his job. As he entered the portal, it began to close. Pargon had almost waited too long.

CHAPTER 1

▼

(THE ROCK)

Tracey was 10 years old and she had a brother named Jason. Jason, who was 8 years old, was always getting into things, weird things, and he always seemed to get Tracey stuck right in the middle of them.

This particular mess actually got started when Tracey and Jason took a trip back to Wisconsin with Mom and Dad. They had driven up to a place called Little Girls Point on Lake Superior for a picnic. Now, that's in Michigan, but they were staying at their aunt's house in Wisconsin, not far away. The park was beautiful, with big shade trees and picnic tables.

"Jason," Tracey said, wide eyed, "I didn't know a lake could be so big! You can't even see the other side."

"Yeah," said Jason, as he fiddled with his slingshot, not even looking up.

The van pulled up to a picnic table near the lake. While Mom and Dad were getting things set up, Tracey and Jason headed for the beach. The beach was covered with really neat rocks and Tracey and Jason were looking for special ones to add to their 'pet rock' collection. Jason was a little ways down the beach from Tracey, digging through some rocks.

"What are you looking for, young man?"

The voice startled Jason. He looked up and squinted. He saw the outline of a man with a cane, the sun almost directly behind him. Jason stood up and shielded his eyes from the sun, trying to get a better view of the man behind the voice. The man wore an old gray suit with a vest and an old gray hat. White hair stuck out from under the hat and Jason could barely see the smiling lips through his fluffy white beard.

"We're looking for rocks for our 'pet rock' collection," replied Jason, still shielding his eyes, squinting and scrunching up his face.

The old man bent down, bringing his face closer to Jason. Around the old man's eyes were wrinkles that seemed to be as old as time itself. But the eyes themselves looked young and seemed to twinkle when the old man talked.

"Why, I used to have great fun doing that when I was a young man. But I only kept the most special ones," said the old man.

"Yeah," said Jason, "me too. The ones I don't like,—I put'em in my slingshot and shoot'em as far out into the lake as I can."

The old man straightened up and laughed. Then he bent down again, looking very serious, his face close to Jason's.

In a soft voice he said, "I'm going to share a little secret with you. Can you keep a secret?"

"Yeah," said Jason and then suddenly realizing he probably couldn't, added, "well, at least I can try."

The old man straightened up and smiled broadly. Then, he looked around.

"In a place like this," he said, "you must look for certain little piles of rocks, that's where the really good ones like to hide. "Suddenly his eyes stopped roving. "There," said the old man, walking a few feet away and pointing his cane at a small pile of rocks. "I'll bet there's a good one hiding in there."

Jason was digging at the pile of rocks almost before the old man had finished the last word. Rocks were flying everywhere as Jason furiously scooped them away with both hands. Then, one caught his eye. It was about the size of a golf ball, mostly covered with mud and dirt. But there was something about it. Jason wiped the mud and dirt off with his hands and then polished it on his shirt.

"Whoa!" exclaimed Jason, "you were right, this is the neatest rock I've ever seen." Jason held the rock up for the old man to inspect.

"Jason," the old man said, "this is a truly wonderful and special rock, why don't you show it to Tracey? I'll bet she would like to see it."

"Yeah," said Jason excitedly, "she'll flip!" and off down the beach he went.

"Tray," Jason yelled. They usually only called each other Tracey or Jason when they were mad or scared or being very formal. The rest of the time, she called him Jay and he called her Tray.

"Look what I found," he yelled.

Tracey was down on her knees, sorting through some rocks. When she saw Jason running down the beach toward her, she stood up and began brushing the dirt off her hands and knees.

"Where did you get it?" asked Tracey.

"That old man helped me find it," said Jason.

Tracey looked around, "What old man?"

"That guy over the———." Jason had cut off the last word because the shoreline was empty as far as the eye could see. "Tray, there was an old man over there a minute ago. He told me where to find it."

"Jason," said Tracey, looking at the rock and shaking her head, "you're getting weird again."

It was the strangest rock they had ever seen. In the sunlight, it sparkled and glowed. They could see into it and through it. It had stripes and swirls in it, like a marble, that seemed to move and twist all by themselves. They knew right away that it was no ordinary rock. There was something very strange and special about it.

"Jay, let me hold it," Tracey said.

They stood there looking into the rock and wondering what it was. They didn't know how long they stood there when they heard Mom calling.

"TRACEY———JASON, TIME FOR LUNCH."

They ran down the beach to where Mom was. They were very excited and Jason held out the rock and said, "Mom, look at this."

Mom took the rock and said, "Oh, what a pretty rock, what are you going to name it?"

"But Mom," said Jason, "this is a special rock, there isn't another rock like it anywhere in the whole world."

Mom smiled and handed the rock back to Jason. "I'm sure there isn't another rock like it anywhere in the whole world," she smiled. She put an arm around both of their shoulders and off they went, down the beach to the picnic table, where Dad was waiting.

"Dad, look at my rock," Jason said excitedly.

Dad took the rock; he looked at it and said, "that's a very nice rock." He handed it back to Jason. "What do you want to drink, lemonade or root beer?"

Dad never got excited about things unless Tracey and Jason were fighting or breaking stuff and then, WATCH OUT.

Tracey and Jason were a little disappointed that Mom and Dad hadn't noticed what a strange rock it really was.

Sometimes grown-ups don't see the same things kids do. Maybe it's because their eyes are older. Tracey and Jason agreed later, they never wanted to get old eyes. Tracey and Jason looked at each other with puzzled faces as Jason shrugged and stuffed the rock in his pocket.

After lunch they played in the park and then went back to their Aunt Grace's house where they were visiting. Aunt Grace was actually Tracey and Jason's Great Aunt. They had never met her until this trip, but she was about the nicest person they had ever met.

That night, when they were getting ready for bed, Jason couldn't find the rock anywhere. Everybody looked but it was nowhere to be found. Jason was sure it had been lost forever. Jason lay in his sleeping bag with tears in his eyes.

"Jay," said Tracey, with sympathy in her voice, "maybe we can find another one just like it."

"There isn't another one like it in the whole world," said Jason, "and I didn't even have a chance to name it."

They had a really neat time on their vacation. Tracey and Jason swam in the lakes and tried water skiing. That didn't work out too well and Tracey got a bruise on her leg from the ski rope.

On the way home they stopped at Yellowstone Park and saw 'Old Faithful'. Tracey and Jason purchased their favorite stuffed animals there. Tracey's was a little brown bear named L'il' Lucas and Jason's was a little brown dog named Hombre. Now, vacations are a lot of fun; but, it's nice to get back home again to your own toys and friends.

CHAPTER 2

▼

(THE PLANE)

The day after they got back, Tracey and Jason were roller skating, while Dad was cleaning out the car. After a trip, Dad always cleaned out the car and Mom always washed clothes and put stuff away.

"Hey kids," Dad called.

They skated over to the car, Jason grabbing hold of the fender and almost falling down.

"Look what I found under one of the car seats," said Dad.

Tracey and Jason's eyes got big.

"Jason, it's your rock," Tracey said.

"My rock, my rock, my little rocky," Jason sang, as he grinned and hugged it to his chest.

"What are you going to name it?" Tracey asked.

Jason stopped smiling and thought, "I'm going to name it," Jason paused,————"Steve," he said, as though he had definitely made up his mind.

"Steve," said Tracey frowning, "Jason, that's a dumb name for a rock."

Jason scrunched up his face and said, "It's my rock and I'll name it whatever I want." Then he stuffed 'Steve', in his pocket and skated off.

When they were done skating, Jason took 'Steve', and put it in one of his dresser drawers where it stayed for several days.

A few days later, Tracey and Jason were making a cardboard airplane in Jason's room. They had some old boxes that they had fastened together and added cardboard wings on the side. The pilot sat in the front box and the passenger in the back box. Tracey was in the front with her bear, Li'l Lucas and Jason was in the back with his dog Hombre. Dad came by the room and looked in.

"What are you gremlins up to now?" he laughed.

"Oh, we just made an airplane," Tracey said.

"Yeah," said Jason, "it doesn't look like much but it's a good one."

"I'm sure it is," smiled Dad, as he looked around the room. "Well, you guys have made an awful mess here. Just make sure you clean it up before you go out to play."

"We will," sang Tracey and Jason at the same time, and they all laughed.

"Tray," said Jason, "it's my turn to be the pilot."

"Oh all right," said Tracey as she got out and got in the back with L'il Lucas, her little brown bear.

Jason started to get in the front with Hombre, his little brown dog, and suddenly stopped.

"Tray," he said, "I'm going to get Steve."

"Jason," said Tracey, a little angry, "we agreed that we were each supposed to have only one animal."

"I know," said Jason, as he ran over to the dresser and took the rock out, "but Steve is a rock, not an animal."

Tracey rolled her eyes back, which she does when she's mad, and slumped back in her seat. Jason got in the front box with Hombre and put Steve in a shoe box they had fastened on the front of the plane for a motor.

The sun was getting higher in the sky. The rays of the sun came through the window to the front of the plane and directly on The Rock named 'Steve'. At first they didn't notice, but after a few minutes they saw the rock start to sparkle and glow. The stripes inside started to twist and the swirls started to twirl. Tracey and Jason sat and watched; their mouths and eyes open wide with astonishment as Steve got brighter and brighter. Suddenly, everything around them started to sparkle and glow a golden color and then there was a flash! The next thing they knew, they were flying through the air, straight toward a mountain.

"Jason!" screamed Tracey, "steer the plane or we'll crash."

Jason took the little cardboard steering wheel and gave it a twist. The little cardboard plane zoomed to the right of the mountain, just brushing the top of some strange kind of giant tree.

They kept zooming in and out and up and down, just missing this and that, until Jason figured out how to make the plane do what he wanted. That's when he started fooling around and really got them in trouble.

"Jason, would you quit fooling around and land this thing?" Tracey yelled.

"Hey Tray, check this out," and then he would swoop up, or down, or right, or left and yell, 'whooooo!!" Well, it didn't take too long before he turned the plane over on its side too far and 'Steve' fell out. Down came the plane, fluttering down into one of those giant trees.

Luckily for Tracey and Jason, the giant tree had big soft limbs and branches, which they were able to grab onto. The little cardboard plane bounced off the branches and fluttered to the ground.

Tracey and Jason pulled themselves up, straddling a big limb, facing each other.

"Jason," said Tracey, talking through her teeth, with fire in her eyes, "now look what you've done."

"Tray," Jason whispered, "look at that."

There was something moving around on the ground.

Chapter 3

▼

(KING WILLIAM)

Down on the ground there was a really big goat with long hair, sniffing and poking around the plane. It was the biggest goat they had ever seen. They quietly climbed down to a branch just above the goat and then Jason sneezed. The goat, startled, looked up.

"What are you doing up in that tree?" asked the goat.

Tracey and Jason, completely startled, sat wide eyed, staring at the goat.

"I said, what are you doing up in that tree?" repeated the goat.

Tracey blinked her eyes and said, "I'm afraid our plane crashed in this tree."

"Hey Tray," said Jason frowning, "goats can't talk."

"I beg your pardon," said the goat. "That may be true for most goats, but this goat can talk. I'm talking aren't I?"

Jason looked at Tracey, scrunched up his face and said, "Tray, goats can't talk."

"I know," Tracey whispered, "but I guess this one can."

"Why don't you come down out of that tree?" said the goat. "It's awfully hard to talk to people when they're sitting in a tree."

As Tracey and Jason climbed down, trying to avoid big balls of sticky sap from the tree, the goat examined the plane.

In an astonished voice, the goat said, "amazing, I never would have thought that something like this would fly. Did you say you call this a —-plane?"

"Yes," answered Tracey, "a plane," as she and Jason started looking around the ground for Hombre and L'il Lucas. They finally found them half-covered with leaves and twigs. Both seemed to have survived the crash all right.

"I'm Tracey and this is my brother Jason," Tracey said to the goat, as she brushed the leaves and twigs off her clothes.

"I am pleased to meet you," said the goat. "I am not really a goat you know, I am actually King William, and you may address me as 'Your Majesty.'"

Jason started laughing so hard he could hardly speak, but finally managed to say, "You don't look like a king to me, you look like a goat. I think I'll call you Billy—-Billy goat." Then Jason rolled on the ground laughing and holding his stomach.

"I'm sorry Your Majesty," apologized Tracey, "my brother is only eight years old and sometimes he can be pretty rude."

King William gave a displeased snort at Jason and then asked Tracey, "How did you get here?"

"There's nothing I'd like more than to tell you how we got here," said Tracey, as she looked around, "but I don't know where we are."

"You don't know where you are?" asked King William with astonishment. "Why, this is the land of CIGAM. At least that's what they call it now. It used to be called MAGIC LAND, but ever since the Evil One took over, everything has been turned around. So instead of MAGIC it's called CIGAM. The Evil One turned me from a King into a goat and banished me on this far-away mountain."

"I'll tell you what happened," said Tracey, "and maybe you can tell me how we can get home."

When Tracey had finished telling King William how they had found the rock and everything that had happened on their vacation, King William asked excitedly, "Where is the rock Jason named 'Steve'? I must see it."

"I don't know where it is now," Tracey said. "It fell out of the plane around here somewhere."

"Quickly," said King William, very excited, "we have to find it."

They looked under the trees and in the grass for a long time when finally, Jason yelled, "Hey Billy, I found it, — I found Steve."

The King rushed over and looked at the rock Jason held in his hand.

"It's The Magic Rock," the King said in a very somber voice. "It's come home."

The King sat on his hind quarters and sighed. "You see," said King William, "many years ago the Evil One had the Magic Rock carried to another land and dropped in a deep watery place where the sun never shines. Because if the sun shines on the Magic Rock and warms it, it will always return to Magic Land according to ancient legend. A storm must have washed it up on shore and covered it with rocks. Jason, when you found it, you put it in your pocket and then lost it under the seat of that thing you call a car. Then, when your father found it, you put it in your pocket again and then in your dresser drawer. The Rock was never in the sunlight long enough to warm it. Finally, when you put it in the sunlight on that contraption you came here in, the sun warmed it, restoring its magical powers and it came home, bringing you with it."

"Then we can use it to fly home again," said Tracey.

"I'm afraid it's not that simple," said King William. "Once The Rock touched the ground of Magic Land, it lost its power until it can again be placed on the Altar of Light."

"Where is that?" asked Jason.

"It is in my castle, far, far to the north," said King William, "where the Evil One now lives. It was magic that brought you here and only magic that can take you home again."

"Then we must go to your castle," said Tracey.

"Yes," said the King, "but I must warn you, it is a long and dangerous journey we may not live to see the end of it. Even if we do, we will still have to face the Evil One when we get there."

They all looked at each other and finally the King said, "I have no choice, I must go to try to win back my kingdom and drive the Evil One out forever."

Tracey looked at Jason then back at King William and said, "We have to go with you. If you don't make it, we're liable to be stuck here forever."

"Yeah," said Jason, "if we don't hurry up, Dad will skin us alive!"

"It is too late to start today," said King William. "We will leave early in the morning. There is a cave near here where we can spend the night and lots of berry bushes nearby."

Tracey and Jason filled themselves with the biggest, juiciest berries they had ever seen and drank water from a sparkling pure brook. Then they followed King William into a huge cave.

"Hey," said Jason, "I don't see any beds in here."

"Well," said King William, "I wasn't exactly expecting guests and this isn't an inn, you know."

Tracey quickly said, "Don't mind my brother, Your Majesty," as she took Jason by the arm and started to pull him out of the cave. "We can gather some grass and leaves for a bed and make ourselves comfortable."

When they were outside, Tracey scowled at Jason and said, "Jason, what is the matter with you, where are your manners? Don't you know that King William is trying to be very nice to us and he is our only hope of getting home?"

Jason had picked up a twig from the ground and began breaking it into little pieces as he leaned against a large rock.

"I suppose you're right Tray, but I don't understand what's going on. We don't know where we are and now we're stuck with some old goat that talks and says he's a King. On top of that, he's mumbling about evil and witch craft and castles. I mean, how do you know that this goat isn't just some wacky old goat?"

"I know," said Tracey, as she walked over and put her arm around Jason's shoulder, "it all seems crazy, but it's getting late and we can talk about it in the morning."

Jason looked at Tracey and smiled.

"You're right Tray", he said, "I'll bet I can get more grass than you can," and they both ran toward the meadow.

CHAPTER 4

▼

(THE JOURNEY
BEGINS)

They slept very well that night. In the morning they ate from the berry bushes and drank from the sparkling stream. The morning was beautiful and from the mountains where they were, they could see out across the valleys and rivers to the dark mountains where the Evil One now lived.

King William looked at them and said, "I must again warn you that this is a very dangerous journey. If you still want to come with me, you must do exactly as I say if you hope to survive."

Tracey and Jason looked at each other for a moment, and then Tracey said, "Our only chance to get home is to go with you and try to help. We'll do what you say."

So, all three started off down the mountain, King William, Tracey and Jason, with Steve, L'il Lucas and Hombre. King

William, being very large and strong, was much faster than Tracey and Jason and had to keep stopping to wait for them.

After a while, King William sighed and said, "this will never do, it will take us a year at this rate."

Tracey and Jason were sitting on a rock trying to catch their breath. "Hey Billy," said Jason, half out of breath, "why don't you let us ride on your back?"

King William gasped, "Ride on my back, —— young man have you completely lost your wits? I am the King."

"Well Billy," said Jason, "if you want to get to your castle before next year, you'd better let us ride on your back."

King William squinted his eyes at Jason and snorted. He stomped around and looked out over the valley.

"Very well," said King William, "but I want you to know that this is the most undignified thing I have ever done. It was embarrassing enough being turned into a goat, and now I'm going to have two children riding around on my back as though I were some stupid mule."

King William walked over and stood next to the rock that Tracey and Jason had climbed up on. They quickly climbed on his back, Tracey in front and Jason in back. He was very easy to ride and down the mountain they went, traveling much faster than before. At lunch time, they again ate the large berries and drank from the sparkling stream they had been following. They climbed on King William's back and continued their journey.

As they rode along, King William said, "We will soon be in the Land of Yuk, so you must stay very close to me at all times."

"Yuk," said Jason, "what's a Yuk?"

"Yuk," said King William, "is a very large snake that loves to eat almost anything and I'm quite sure he would love to make a meal out of you. He will not bother me because I am too large to swallow, and also because I'm bewitched. If you eat something that is bewitched, it leaves a very bad taste in your mouth. The only exception is rabbits, or so I'm told."

CHAPTER 5

▼

(THE LAND OF YUK)

The late afternoon sun felt good as they traveled down the mountain. It would not be long before they would have to find a place to spend the night.

Suddenly there came a sound from just around the next bend in the path. It was a loud hissing sound that brought goose bumps to their skin. King William crept quietly to a spot where they could peek around the corner. Not far off the path was an enormous snake, and it had its tail wrapped around a furry, little white rabbit.

"It is Yuk," whispered King William. "He can't see very well, but his other senses are keen, or he wouldn't have been able to catch that poor little rabbit."

"Ssssst, and now for my lunch," said Yuk in an icy, hissing voice. Yuk opened his mouth wide and leaned toward the little white rabbit. Suddenly there was a snapping sound from behind Tracey. A rock shot like a bullet and hit Yuk on the left side of the head.

"There's your lunch," yelled Jason as he still held his slingshot outstretched in his hand.

Yuk's head drooped and a quiver went through his body. The little rabbit wiggled free and scampered into the woods. In a moment, Yuk had regained his senses, but a large lump was already forming over his left eye. Yuk's eyes turned red as he shook with anger.

"Ssssstt, who dares attack me in my own kingdom?" hissed Yuk.

"It is your King," said King William, as he moved further down the path.

"Hisssssst, you are not my king," hissed YUK. "Sssssst, this is my land and I am the, sssst, King here."

"This is all my land," said King William, "and you know it, Yuk."

A hissing laugh came from Yuk as he said, "I think my friend ssst the Evil One, ssst, has taken your place."

"Not for long," yelled Tracey, "we are going to put the Magic Rock back on the Altar of Light and drive the Evil One away."

Yuk pulled back in surprise. "Ssssst, you have the Magic Rock? Sssst, you will never succeed. Sssst, you will never leave here alive." As Yuk started to slither down toward them, "Sssssst, you will die."

"Hang on," King William yelled to Tracey and Jason, as he ran down the path, just outside the reach of Yuk. Tracey and Jason grabbed tightly to King William's hair and hung on for their lives. As they ran away from Yuk, they could hear him hissing with anger.

"Hisssst, you will not escape, sssst, you will DIE."

When they were safely away from Yuk, King William slowed to a walk.

"For the next two days," said King William, "we will be in Yuk's land. We must choose carefully where we sleep so that Yuk can't sneak up on us in the middle of the night. And, above all, you must both stay very close to me."

After about an hour of winding down the mountain and putting some distance between them and Yuk, King William stopped.

"There is a place where we can spend the night." he said. It was a small hill, flat on top and about thirty feet high. It was very steep on all four sides except where there was a rugged path going up to the top.

"If we pile sharp rocks in the path." said King William, "Yuk will not cross them and the sides are too steep for him to climb."

They quickly ate some of the giant berries from the bushes that grew along the nearby stream. They were a long way ahead of Yuk, but they nervously kept a close watch anyway. Tracey and Jason found rocks with the sharpest points they could find and piled them across the path with the points sticking up. When the King was satisfied that they were safe, they climbed to the top of the hill to find a comfortable place to sleep.

However, the rocks were too hard for Tracey and Jason to get comfortable. It didn't bother King William, who seemed quite comfortable with all his hair.

"Tracey, this is ridiculous," said Jason, totally frustrated. Jason grabbed Hombre, climbed up on a rock and dove down on King William's stomach. King William's eyes popped open and a woof of air came out his mouth. King William lifted his head and glared at Jason.

"Young man," said King William, angrily, "what do you think you are doing?"

Jason sat up and said, "Look Billy, Tracey and I aren't goats."

"No kidding," said the King, "but I'm not a goat either, I am the King and it is not dignified for people to be jumping all over the King."

"You might be a King," said Jason, "but right now you're a goat with a lot of hair. You have a built-in bed and I think you ought to share it."

"Good grief," moaned King William, as he lay his head back down. "All right, all right, ——I'm too tired to argue." King William lifted his head again and glared at Jason, "But if I roll over in the middle of the night and SQUASH you, don't blame me." King William laid his head back down and closed his eyes.

"What about Tracey?" asked Jason.

"Yes, Tracey too," sighed King William, his eyes still closed.

Tracey quickly grabbed L'il Lucas and climbed up on the rock. Kings William's eyes again popped open and he quickly lifted his head, yelling, "But don't jump." It was too late; Tracey was already in the air.

Whoosh, went the air out of King William as she landed squarely on his stomach.

CHAPTER 6

▼

(SIR GEORGE)

The sun had not come up yet, but soon it would be peeping over the horizon. Jason turned over and felt for Hombre. When he couldn't find him, he sat up, rubbed the sleep out of his eyes and looked around. In the night, Hombre must have rolled off the king and lay on the ground not far from the ledge.

"Boy, it's a good thing Hombre didn't fall over the edge," Jason mumbled to himself. He climbed down off King William and sleepily walked over to where Hombre lay on the ground. Jason reached down but accidentally knocked Hombre over the edge.

"Darn," whispered Jason disgusted with himself. It was light enough that Jason could see Hombre lying at the bottom of the hill. Jason looked around. There was nothing in sight. He ran down the path to where the sharp rocks lay and looked around once more. "The coast is clear," he whispered to himself. Jason climbed over the rocks and ran around the hill to where Hombre lay on the ground. He picked him up and brushed him off. "Not a scratch on him," Jason whispered, as he smiled to himself. As Jason turned to go back to the path, something wrapped around him and squeezed him so hard he couldn't make a sound. There was a hissing laugh, "Hsssst, now you are mine," hissed Yuk.

The morning sun had just peeped over the horizon, when Tracey woke up. She sat up, stretched and yawned. Tracey noticed Jason was gone. "Jason," she called softly, so she wouldn't disturb King William. Tracey climbed down and looked around. "Jason," she called a little louder, causing King William to stir in his sleep. There was no answer, only silence. Tracey ran over and shook King William's head.

"King William, wake up," said Tracey with panic in her voice, "Jason is gone."

The King quickly stood up, shaking his head and blinking his eyes. "What?" he said, still half asleep.

Tracey was frantic, "I said Jason is gone, we've got to find him."

They quickly searched the top of the hill and then looked over the edge. Suddenly, Tracey spotted something. At the bottom of the hill lay Hombre and Jason's slingshot.

"Hurry," Tracey said with urgency, as she ran toward the path, "down at the bottom of the hill."

"Be careful," cried King William as he trotted after Tracey, "Yuk may be down there."

Tracey picked up Hombre and Jason's slingshot. She looked all over and called his name as loud as she could. The tears were streaming down her face. King William was beside her now. The King saw the marks in the dirt and sat down on his hind quarters.

Sadly he said, "Tracey," he paused, — "Yuk has been here, I'm afraid that Jason————," and then he stopped and hung his head.

Tracey put her arms around King William's neck and cried.

"We've got to do something," she cried, "we've got to do something."

King William, his head still hung sadly, said, "I'm afraid it may be too late, I don't think that there is anything we can do."

There was a rustling in the bushes nearby. Tracey and King William turned quickly. King William narrowed his eyes and snorted angrily. He knew he couldn't win a fight with Yuk, but he was mad enough to try. The bushes rustled again and out hopped a furry little white rabbit. It was the same rabbit that they had saved from Yuk.

"Who are you?" asked the rabbit.

Tracey and King William were both taken by surprise.

"The rabbit can talk," said Tracey with tears still in her eyes.

After a moment, King William stood up as straight as a goat can stand, looked as dignified as a goat can look and spoke in as distinguished a voice as a goat can have.

"I am King William, rightful ruler of all this land."

The rabbit hopped up in front of King William, bowed his head and said, "Your Majesty, I am Sir George."

"Sir George," gasped King William, "you were always one of my most faithful Knights. My old friend, I thought you were dead."

"And we thought you were dead," said Sir George. "The Evil One has turned all of your faithful subjects into different kinds of animals, which are hunted and killed by her evil subjects. All of your loyal Knights have been turned into rabbits and Yuk hunts us down for pleasure. If it had not been for the boy, I would have been only another meal for Yuk," said Sir George.

Tracey hung her head and sniffed, "That was my brother Jason," she said sadly, the tears coming back into her eyes. "But Yuk has eaten him."

"No," said Sir George, "since the time you saved my life, I have followed you. Yuk has carried your brother off to some caves near here. He doesn't like to eat in the morning if he can help it. He would rather eat in the early afternoon. There is still time to save him."

Tracey wiped the tears out of her eyes and smiled happily, "Jason is all right," she said.

King William sighed and sat down, "But what can we do?" he said.

"Your Majesty," said Sir George, "there is no other meal that Yuk would rather have than a fat juicy rabbit. Jason saved my life. The least I can do is to save his. I suggest that you trade me for Jason."

"Sir George," said king William, "you have always been my noblest and finest Knight." The King walked around for a minute and finally said, "If only we could think of another way."

"Wait a minute," said Tracey, "I have an idea."

"Ssssst, and now for my dinner," said Yuk, sitting in front of a cave with his tail wrapped around Jason. His mouth opened wide, ready to make a meal out of Jason, when suddenly he was startled.

"Yuk," he heard someone call loudly, "you don't want to eat that boy."

Yuk hissed loudly, "Sssst, who is foolish enough to interrupt my dinner?"

The King said, "It is I, King William."

"You are not my King," hissed Yuk, "and you will not interrupt my meal. Now it is time to eat." He turned back to Jason and started to open his mouth.

"That boy will leave a bad taste in your mouth, Yuk," said King William. "You have never eaten a boy before and I am told that they do not taste good."

"Sssst, you take me for a fool," said Yuk. "Do you expect me to let this boy go when I am hungry? Sssst, enough of this nonsense, it is time to eat."

"But we have caught you a fine, fat rabbit," said Tracey, "we will trade you for the boy."

"What?" said Yuk. Rabbit was his favorite meal and his mouth started to water. It was true; a rabbit would be so delicious right now. "Sssst show me the rabbit," said Yuk, trying to contain his excitement.

Tracey held up the rabbit tied on a vine.

Yuk's eyes were not good, but he could see the soft fur. The wind was in the right direction and he could smell rabbit.

"Sssst, why should I trade you?" asked Yuk.

"Because the boy was so easy to catch," said King William. "I'm sure you could easily catch him again. You could have the boy anytime but rabbits are much harder to catch and so tasty."

Yuk could resist no longer. "All right," said Yuk, "bring the rabbit to me."

"Now you must think that we are fools," said King William. "If we bring the rabbit to you, you will eat the rabbit and the boy."

"Hsssttt," Yuk hissed angrily.

"We will tie the rabbit to that tree near the cave," said King William. "When you can see that the rabbit is tied, you can let the boy go."

It was plain that Yuk was angry, but he agreed. Yuk could wait no longer for something to eat. Yuk saw Tracey carry the rabbit over and tie him to the tree. When Yuk was satisfied that the rabbit was tied up, he let Jason go. Jason ran as fast as he could, his eyes wide with fright, to where Tracey and King William waited nearby. Even before Jason got to Tracey and the King, Yuk was upon his meal. His mighty mouth opened wide and came down on the poor helpless rabbit. Yuk hissed in anger as he twisted and shook. Jason didn't know what was happening as Tracey and King William started laughing so hard that Tracey, holding her stomach, fell to her knees and King William rolled over on his side. Then, from out of the bushes hopped Sir George, he was missing a considerable amount of his fur.

Tracey, still laughing so hard she had tears in her eyes, hugged her brother and explained to him what they had done. They had collected a ball of the thick sticky sap from one of the giant trees, like the one they had landed in. Then they had pulled out some of Sir George's fur and stuck it to the sap so Yuk would think it was a rabbit. The trick had worked and now Yuk's mouth was stuck almost completely shut and he had sap and fur stuck all over him. When Jason found out what had happened, he started to laugh too. Everybody was laughing except for poor Sir George, who had big bald spots all over his body. Sir George sat there, angrily thumping one of his rear feet on the ground.

"I suppose you think it's funny." said Sir George, "but it wasn't your fur that was pulled out."

This made him even more disgusted because it made everyone laugh even louder.

Finally King William got to his feet and said, still chuckling, "Don't worry Sir George, your fur will grow back."

When the laughter was almost over, they decided they had better start off down the mountain.

"Wait a minute," said Jason. Jason quickly found a nice sized rock and put it in the slingshot Tracey had brought with her. "Hey Yuk," he yelled, "you look funny with that lump on one side of your head." Then he quickly let the rock fly, neatly placing it on the other side of Yuk's head. Yuk, his mouth stuck together, groaned as his eyes crossed and he rolled over on his side. Almost immediately, another lump started to come up on his head.

"There." yelled Jason, "matching lumps." They all began laughing again.

Chapter 7

---▼---

(BEING FOLLOWED)

It was now late afternoon and the sun shown brightly, except far to the north, where the dark clouds hung ominously over the mountains. At least they wouldn't have to worry about Yuk for quite a while. Tracey and Jason climbed up on top of King William's back and off they went, Sir George hopping along next to them. This brightened Sir George's spirits greatly as he chuckled about Tracey and Jason riding on the King's back.

King William glared at Sir George and said, "Hold your tongue, you bald rabbit."

Before the sun set, they found a safe place to camp. It was near a babbling brook and there were lots of big juicy berries. When they had finished eating, they built a small fire and watched the sun set over the valley.

"Our journey will take us there," said King William, pointing his nose at a vast expanse of nothing, stretching almost to the mountains. "It is called the endless desert. It will not be an easy journey and there are many dangers but if we take enough water, we should be all right."

"But first," said Sir George, "we must cross the canyon tomorrow."

"Yes," said King William, "and let us hope that the old wooden bridge is still safe to cross."

A little snort startled them and they turned quickly, only to see Jason sitting Indian style, with his back against a rock, his arms at his sides, his head tilted forward, sleeping. They all chuckled as they relaxed.

"I guess I'm a little jumpy," said Tracey.

"We all are," said King William, smiling, "and I think we had all better get some sleep."

Tracey woke Jason and they again made beds out of grass and twigs near the fire. Soon they were all asleep. All that is, except for Sir George, who sat nervously, his ears twitching, looking out into the darkness. He had found the king and these two precious children. For the first time in many months, he had hope and something to live for. So, Sir George would sit this night and watch, to make sure they were safe.

Jason was the first one to wake in the morning. He laid absolutely still, his eyes wide with fear as he heard a growling sound behind him. Tracey and Jason were sleeping in opposite directions with their heads only a little ways apart. Very slowly Jason reached out and shook Tracey's head gently.

"Tracey," he whispered. Tracey's eyes started to open. "Tracey, don't move and don't make a sound," he whispered.

Tracey, awake now, whispered back, "What's the matter?"

"I think there's a lion or bear or something behind us," whispered Jason. "Can you hear him?"

Tracey listened, "Yes," she whispered back. They lay there for a long time before Tracey whispered, "how long has he been growling like that?"

"Ever since I woke up," whispered Jason.

"I'm going to look," whispered Tracey.

"No," whispered Jason excitedly, "If you move he'll see us and get us."

Tracey slowly lifted her head and began to turn it. Jason closed his eyes and scrunched up his face, waiting to be pounced on.

Suddenly Tracey sat up and in a loud voice said, "Jason, you idiot, you scared the daylights out of me."

Jason opened his eyes but lay still.

Mimicking Jason in a baby's voice Tracey said, "Tracey, there's a lion or bear behind us." Then she returned to her normal angry voice. "Well, look ding dong," as she got to her feet and started brushing the grass and twigs off herself. "Go ahead, look at the lion."

Jason sat up and looked. There was Sir George, leaning up against a tree, snoring up a storm. Jason stood up, with a sheepish grin on his face, and started brushing the grass and twigs off his clothes.

"Tray," said Jason, "I knew all the time it was Sir George, I was just playing a game with you."

Tracey put her hands on her hips and glared at Jason. "Right," said Tracey angrily, "uh huh, so you knew it was Sir George! Jason, you did not, and you know you didn't. You're just telling stories again."

About this time, King William jumped to his feet and shook his head, trying to wake up.

"What on earth is going on here? What is the racket?" he asked.

"I'm sorry about all the noise, King William," said Tracey, "but Jason is imagining monsters. He thought Sir George was a lion or something."

They all looked over and there was Sir George, still leaning up against the tree and still snoring and snorting up a storm.

"Hey Tray," said Jason, with a puzzled look on his face, "is that the way a rabbit is supposed to sleep, leaning up against a tree?"

"I don't know", said Tracey, "I don't think so; it does seem kind of strange".

"No," said King William, "although this place is safe, Sir George, as tired as he was, tried to stay awake all night to keep watch for us."

King William looked quietly for a moment at his loyal friend, Sir George. Then said, "We'll let him sleep awhile and leave later in the morning."

"Hey Willie," said Jason, "I appreciate having something to eat but don't they have something to eat around here but berries?"

"Oh, so it's Willie now," replied King William, "is there no end to the names your creative little brain is going to come up with?"

Jason sat thoughtfully for a moment, and then replied "I don't know," then with a smile, "we'll just have to wait and see."

King William snorted with displeasure, "Well, just so you know, as we get further down the mountain there well be various fruit trees, something new for you to gnaw on—until then, it's berries."

Tracey and Jason gently carried Sir George over and laid him on one of the beds of grass and leaves.

They ate juicy berries and drank from the sparkling brook. Tracey and Jason climbed up on a large rock that had a good view of the valley below. The early morning sun was warm and felt good. Jason had his little dog Hombre and a pile of small rocks that were just the right size for his slingshot. Every so often he would shoot at a tree or a branch or a rock. The sun moved a little higher in the sky and Jason finally ran out of rocks, but didn't want to climb down for more. Tracey lay on the rock with her eyes closed. Her little brown bear, L'il Lucas, was on her stomach. Jason sat on the rock looking out over the valley.

Without looking at Tracey, Jason said, "Tray?" and waited to see if she was asleep.

"Yes?" Tracey answered, without opening her eyes.

"I wonder what Mom and Dad are doing right now?" said Jason.

Tracey lay there for a moment and then sat up. They looked at each other and then Tracey said, with a tear in her eye, "Jay, I was just thinking the same thing."

Jason looked out over the valley again and said, "This whole thing seems like a dream, but every morning I wake up and we're still here."

"Look Jay," Tracey said, "I know we're going to get out of this OK. By the way, I'm sorry I got so mad at you when you thought Sir George was a lion."

Jason looked at Tracey and smiled. "That's OK, big sister, it was kind of stupid."

Just then, they heard King William calling them. They scrambled down off the rock and ran back to the campsite. Sir George was up, stretching and yawning.

"I'm sorry I've held you up," said Sir George.

"Don't apologize, my old friend," said King William, "but it is mid-morning and we must continue our journey."

They traveled the winding path down the mountain, stopping occasionally to rest. It was noon and Tracey and Jason were eating berries down by the stream.

"Your Majesty," said Sir George quietly, "I am almost certain we are being followed."

"I would be very surprised if it were Yuk," said King William with a smile, "I doubt if he is even close to finishing the last meal we gave him." Then he became serious, "Who do you think it might be?"

"I'm not sure," said Sir George, "but when we leave, I will hide in those rocks down around the bend and wait."

"Be very careful, my friend," said King William, with a concerned look on his face.

When they had all finished eating, Tracey and Jason again climbed on King William's back and they continued on. As they went around the bend, Tracey and Jason didn't notice Sir George slip quickly into the rocks. It couldn't have been more than a couple of minutes later and the air was filled with screeches and yaps.

King William yelled for Tracey and Jason to hang on as he quickly turned and ran up the path. As they approached the commotion, they could see Sir George was holding a small dog down on the ground and was thumping him with one of his rear feet. King William rushed up to Sir George and seeing that he didn't need any help, said, "That's enough, Sir George."

As Sir George got off the little dog, the little dog spoke. "You're Sir George?" asked the little dog.

They all stood in amazement, staring at the dog. The little dog slowly got to his feet. He was unhurt but covered with dirt. While he was shaking the dirt off, he said, "I'm Squire Josh."

"Squire Josh," said Sir George with amazement, "I'm sorry lad, if I knew who you were, I never would have jumped you." Suddenly, Sir George became very formal. "Squire Josh, this is King William."

Squire Josh immediately bowed his head, saying with great excitement, "Your Majesty, it's too good to be true."

"Squire Josh," said King William, "this is Tracey and Jason. They have brought the Magic Rock back to us, so now you

know where we are going. Because this journey is so dangerous, as your King, I will not order you to go, but I will ask
you, will you join us?"

"Your Majesty," said Squire Josh, bowing again, "to serve
you and Sir George again would be a great honor."

"By the way," said Sir George, "what was that you were carrying in your mouth?"

"Sir George," said Squire Josh, "that was your knife. As a
small dog, I was not big enough to steal your sword from the
Evil One, but I did steal your knife. I've carried it with me all
these months, hoping to find you."

They found the knife almost buried in the soft dirt. Tracey
and Jason helped to tie the knife to the side of Sir George. As a
rabbit, of course, he couldn't use it but it did make him look a
little more official and it made him feel more like a Knight of
the Kingdom again.

▼

CHAPTER 8

(THE BOTTOMLESS CANYON)

It was late afternoon as they traveled the trail toward the canyon. Tracey and Jason were riding on King William's back and Squire Josh, the little dog, trotted along beside them. Sir George had gone ahead to check on the bridge. Jason thought the constant clip-pity-clop of the hoofs was getting boring, so he decided to sing.

"Old McDonald had a farm, ee ey, ee ey, ooh, and on that farm he had a goat, ee ey, ee ey ooh."

Squire Josh was doing his best not to laugh.

King William came to a dead stop and turned his head to look at Jason.

"Look, young man," said King William, "it's undignified enough to have two children riding around on my back, and to be called Billy, instead of King William, without someone singing songs about me being some sort of a farm animal."

Jason chuckled, "Sorry Billy——I mean King Billy," laughed Jason. "Would you like me to sing something else?"

Squire Josh was not able to completely control his laughter. He was kind of snickering and snorting.

King William started off down the path again, giving a disapproving glance at Squire Josh. "I'd rather that you didn't sing at all, but if you must sing, sing something other than that," said King William.

Jason laughed and started singing again. "Oh, the old gray Billy goat ain't what he used to be, ain't what he used to be, ain't what he used to be."

"Good grief," groaned King William, as Jason laughed.

"How about this one?" laughed Jason. "Four and twenty Billy goats baked in a pie?"

As Jason laughed, King William looked back at Tracey and asked, "How often does your brother get in these moods?"

"I'm afraid it's much too often, Your Majesty," said Tracey, rolling her eyes toward the top of her head.

By this time, Squire Josh had dashed off the road and they could hear hysterical laughter coming from behind one of the rocks. Finally, about five minutes later, Squire Josh caught up with them again, still chuckling from time to time.

Suddenly, Sir George came racing up the trail, his long ears flat against his body. He skidded to a stop in front of King William and sat panting for a moment.

"Your Majesty," he said breathlessly, "the Evil One must know that you are coming. Ikar, King of the rats, and hundreds of his followers are guarding this side of the bridge."

Squire Josh hung his head and slowly shook it back and fourth. "There is no way we can get past them," he said.

Tracey and Jason climbed down off the King's back and King William sat down. After a long moment, King William said, "We had better find a safe place to camp for the night and try to think of something."

The mood in camp that night was very sullen. Sir George explained the exact layout of the bridge and Ikar's camp. No one had any good ideas. It soon became late and time for bed. Since they couldn't risk a camp fire, Tracey and Jason had to sleep on King William's stomach and cover up with his long hair. When King William heard a little chuckle from Sir George and Squire Josh, he looked at them and said in a threatening voice, "So help me, if we survive and either one of you breathe one word of this to anyone, I'll have your hides."

"Oh, I wouldn't breathe a word, Your Majesty," said Sir George. "Nor I," said Squire Josh, both laughing. Then at the same time they said, "Not a word."

The sun had not quite risen when Tracey felt something gently shaking her. She heard an excited voice whispering, "Tray, wake up Tray, I have an idea."

Tracey looked around with her eyes half open and said, "Jay, it isn't even morning yet, what do you want?"

"Tray," Jason said, still very excited, "do you remember all those old Westerns I used to watch on TV?"

"Jason," said Tracey, still half asleep, "this is no time to be talking about old Westerns on television. Now go back to sleep."

Tracey turned over and laid down again, but Jason shook her.

"Tray, wake up, I have an idea," Jason said shaking her again.

"Oh, all right," said Tracey, as she sat up, tired and irritated. "Tell me about your old Western, so I can get some sleep."

About this time, King William lifted up his head.

"What on earth are you two doing, bouncing around on my stomach and yelling at this time of the morning?"

Sir George, suddenly awakened by the noise, began bouncing around the camp yelling, "Guards to the front, archers ready, swordsmen, lop off their heads. Let no one enter the castle." Tracey, Jason and King William watched Sir George in astonishment. Then Squire Josh, waking up suddenly, began running around the camp yapping.

Finally, King William said, "Sir George," then louder, "SIR GEORGE."

Sir George stopped and looked around, regaining his wits.

"Sir George," said King William, "we're not under attack."

Sir George narrowed his eyes, started twitching his ears and with a disgusted look on his face said, "Well then, what's all the racket?"

"I'm afraid," said Tracey, "that all the racket is my brother. He has some idea that couldn't wait until later."

"This better be good," said Sir George, thumping one of his hind feet on the ground.

"I was trying to tell Tray," said Jason excitedly, "when the rest of you woke up, that I used to watch a lot of old Westerns on TV."

"Wait a minute," said King William, still a little sleepy, "what's an old Western on TV?"

Tracey, still a little angry at being awakened, said, "Jason, they don't have old Westerns or TV here. Just tell us what your idea is."

"Well," said Jason, trying to control his excitement, "if somebody was holed up in a cabin or a barn at the bottom of the hill, the other guys would light a wagon on fire and push it down the hill so they would have to run out of the way."

King William yawned, "What's that got to do with us?"

"The path to the bridge," said Jason, "is downhill, so we can do the same thing to Ikar and the rest of the rats."

"One problem," said Sir George, "we don't have a wagon."

"No we don't," said Jason, "but we could tie a big ball of grass and brush together, light it on fire and roll it down the hill. We can follow behind it and when they run out of the way, we can run across the bridge."

They were all awake now and their brains were thinking.

After a little while, King William said, "It might work, but even if we got across the bridge, we would still have hundreds of rats following right behind us."

"That's right," said Sir George, "and with Ikar leading them, it wouldn't take long for them to run us down."

"Wait a minute," said Tracey, "didn't you say the bridge was made out of wood?"

"Yes," said King William.

"Then," said Tracey, "we can tie a smaller bundle of brush on a vine; light it on fire and drag it behind King William."

"And when we cross the bridge," cried Squire Josh, excitedly, "we can drop the vine, blocking and burning the bridge."

"Right," said Tracey, clapping her hands and jumping up and down.

"Right on," yelled Jason, jumping up and down with his arms stretched above his head.

"I'm happy," said King William, "for old Westerns on TV, ——whatever it is."

They spent all day collecting the driest brush and twigs they could find. They used green vines to tie them together into a very large ball. Some other vines, they tied into a bundle to drag behind King William. Late in the afternoon, they rolled the big ball near the top of the hill where the path sloped down toward the bridge. They peered over the rocks and saw hundreds of rats camped out by the bridge.

"We're in luck," said Sir George, "they're still all on this side of the bridge."

"And they're so sure of themselves," said King William, "That they haven't even placed guards up here on the hill."

The canyon was only about 200 feet wide where the bridge stretched across it, but it quickly got wider on both sides and stretched as far as the eye could see. It was so deep that Sir George said it was named The Bottomless Canyon.

The path went straight down the hill, where it angled left at a large boulder, just before it went across the bridge.

The second pile of brush that they had collected would be tied to King William's tail and dragged behind them. When they crossed the bridge, Jason would pull on the end of the vine he was holding, releasing it on the bridge.

"When shall we go?" asked Sir George.

"We will go when it is dark and most of the rats are asleep," said King William. "That way, the confusion will have most of them disoriented, hopefully, long enough for us to get across the bridge."

None of them could sleep, but they all rested quietly. Sir George and Squire Josh took turns keeping watch.

It was a dark, moonless night. They had rolled the big ball of brush to the top of the hill. They could see dozens of small camp fires, all on this side of the bridge. King William stood a few feet behind the big ball of brush, with Tracey and Jason on his back. Tracey rode toward the front and Jason toward the back, holding the end of the vine. The vine ran from King William's tail to the other pile of brush. Jason had strapped on Sir George's knife so Sir George could run faster.

"You children hold on tight," said King William.

"We will," they both said at the same time.

"It's time," nodded King William to Sir George and Squire Josh.

They lit two torches and Sir George lit the big ball in front, while Squire Josh lit the pile of brush in the back. Sir George gave the big ball a little push and it started to roll down the hill, bursting quickly into flames. King William, with Sir

George and Squire Josh on either side of him, began to trot, then gallop and finally run after the speeding ball of fire. They were into the rats now, who were screaming and shrieking. The rats were bumping into each other and clamoring to get out of the way, as if they were being pursued by fiery demons from the underworld. One of the rats had managed to run in and jump on the back of Squire Josh. Jason swung his sling-shot down; catching the rubber band around the rat's neck, throwing him off and under the pile of burning brush King William was dragging. Another rat dashed in, trying to bite King William's leg, but Sir George lowered his head and with a mighty push from his hind legs, butted the rat, sending him rolling under the hoofs of King William. The big ball of fire slammed into the boulder near the bridge, exploding fire and sparks in all directions like a giant fireworks display.

In the light from the exploding ball, Tracey saw Ikar sitting on a ledge. His face was hideous and distorted. His sharp teeth were bared and his eyes glowed red in the light from the fire as he screamed orders for the rats to attack. However, the confusion was too great and it would all be over before the rats knew what hit them.

King William made a quick left to go over the bridge, taking them straight through the fire from the exploding brush ball. When he made the quick left, Jason lost Hombre. In an attempt to save Hombre, Jason dropped the end of the vine he had been holding. Before Hombre hit the ground, Squire Josh caught him in his teeth, hardly missing a step. They were on the bridge now.

"Jason, release the vine," yelled King William.

Jason had turned himself around and was holding tightly to King William with both legs, pulling at King William's tail, trying desperately to get a hold of the vine. They were half way across now.

"Hurry," screamed Tracey, "we don't have much time."

Jason couldn't reach it. They were 3/4 of the way across now. Jason pulled out Sir George's knife and with a mighty hack, cut the vine. King William let out a hoot and took off like a shot. Jason looked back and saw the bundle of burning brush and the end of the vine he had cut, laying on the bridge and ————oh,oh, a little piece off the end of King William's tail. The bridge was old and dry, so it didn't take long before it was fully engulfed in flames.

Tracey bandaged the end of King William's tail the best she could, but it's not easy to bandage the end of a tail. They walked quietly down the dark road, King William occasionally switching his sore tail and snorting. This was accompanied by soft chuckles from Sir George and Squire Josh.

When it was light enough, they would find a safe place to sleep and rest. Ikar and the rats were now safely behind them.

CHAPTER 9

▼

(SPIDER LAKE)

The next four days were about as uneventful as could be expected, with Jason along. Jason got into an argument the first day with Sir George because Jason didn't want to give Sir George his knife back. Jason told Sir George he had two built-in knives with those two big buck teeth of his and besides, what's a floppy eared rabbit going to do with a knife? Sir George explained that when he regained his form, he was personally going to stick that knife in the evil one. Finally, King William intervened and took Sir George's side. King William explained that it made him more than a little nervous, and for good reason, as he switched his sore tail back and forth, to have Jason carrying the knife around. Perhaps———when Jason got a little older? So Jason found a piece of wood that looked like a small baseball bat and started carrying that around, ready to whack any evil-looking thing that might appear.

The trail wound and curved, always making its way downward. The stream that they had been following before they had gotten to the bridge had ended in a beautiful waterfall into the Bottomless Canyon. However, there was another stream to follow now. The weather got warmer the lower they went and the closer they got to the endless desert. The second day was uneventful, which was a pleasant surprise for King William. The third day, however, was a little different.

They had stopped about noon to eat and drink. Tracey was talking to Squire Josh and King William had sat down to rest. Suddenly, there was a commotion back in the rocks. When King William, Tracey and Squire Josh got there, Sir George was angrily yelling at Jason.

"You did this on purpose, because I wouldn't let you have the knife," yelled Sir George.

"I did not," said Jason, trying to control his laughter, "I didn't even know you were back there."

Jason was coming down off a big rock, zipping up his pants. Sir George was sitting there, floppy eared and dripping wet.

"I just climbed up on that rock to go to the bathroom," explained Jason, still laughing "I didn't know he was behind the rock."

"You did too know I was there," yelled Sir George. Then turning to the rest of us he said, angrily, "He wet on me, can you believe it? He wet on me."

Squire Josh was trying not to laugh; Tracey was holding her breath and turning red, trying not to laugh. King William——————he was laughing.

Sir George took a long bath in the stream and they left.

Stretching almost as far as the eye could see was the endless desert. On the horizon, just before the mountains which were covered with black clouds, they could barely see a haze from the dark forest and the death swamp. Tomorrow they would be at the bottom and the last water they would find until they reached Crystal Springs, about halfway across the desert. But tomorrow, —————tomorrow they would stop and rest at Spider Lake.

The journey to the bottom of the mountain was almost over. For the last two hours, they had been able to catch glimpses of Spider Lake. It wasn't a very big lake, but it looked crystal clear with a sky-blue tint. The weather had become noticeably warmer, as the trail they had been following began to flatten out. As they headed toward the lake, the surrounding area took on an almost park like setting. The whole area was covered with large oak trees, spread a comfortable distance apart. Their large leafy arms stretched out, providing cooling shade for them and homes for the birds and other creatures.

"Why do they call it Spider Lake?" asked Tracey.

"Because," said King William, "there is a colony of large spiders that have made this side of the lake their home."

"Big spiders?" said Tracey, nervously looking around. "Wait a minute; I don't even like little spiders, let alone big spiders."

"Don't worry," said King William laughing. "These spiders have always been very friendly and loyal to me and my subjects."

"Look," said Squire Josh, trotting along next to them, "there's one of the spiders now."

A spider up ahead spotted them and quickly ran up into one of the huge oak trees. The spider was black and the body was about the size of a basketball.

"That's strange," said Sir George, "they've never acted that way before."

"They probably don't know who we are," said King William. "We don't exactly look like ourselves."

They could see the lake just up ahead now, but no more spiders. It was late afternoon when they reached the edge of the shore. The water was crystal clear and cool. They drank the water and ate berries off the bushes that grew near the lake. When it started getting dark, they made a campfire near the lake.

"I doubt that there is anything wrong", said King William, "but I think we should take turns keeping watch, while the rest sleep."

Tracey was wide awake, so she took the first watch. The little waves from the lake made peaceful lapping sounds on the shore. The stars twinkled brightly in the moonless night sky. Everything seemed peaceful— almost too peaceful. Tracey watched the dark woods, straining to see or hear anything that might signal danger. The flickering camp fire was casting eerie shadows among the trees, reminding her of ghost stories she had heard. When Tracey's watch was up, she woke Squire Josh and sat with him for awhile, talking, while her eyes strained to see into the darkness. Finally, she laid down by the campfire and drifted off to sleep. When Tracey woke in the morning, she felt foolish that she had worried so much.

The morning was beautiful and sunny. It was a little warm but they all knew it was much cooler than the desert was going to be. They again drank the cool water and ate the berries. There was still no sign of the spiders. It seemed King William was right, the spiders were peaceful and maybe even a little shy.

"We'll need to take some water with us when we enter the Endless Desert," said King William.

"King Billy," said Jason, "I thought you said that Crystal Springs was only half way across."

"It is," said Sir George answering, "but it is still a three day journey to Crystal Springs."

"There are some gourds that grow near here," said King William. "We need to find some suitable ones that we can use to carry water and berries in for our journey."

They found several gourds and cleaned them out. They filled most of them with water and strapped them across King William's back, with some vines. When they were done, King William had eight water gourds strapped on and Tracey and Jason had one gourd each, strapped to their backs, containing berries. With Tracey and Jason on King William's back, it was a heavy load, but King William was strong and didn't complain.

"It's time to go," said King William. He looked around, "Has anybody seen Squire Josh?" he asked.

Suddenly there was a barking and yelping coming from under one of the large oak trees. A web had fallen over Squire

Josh and a large black spider was coming out of the tree. Squire Josh tried desperately to escape the web, but it was no use. King William, with his heavy load, could not move quickly enough. Sir George was off and running toward the little dog, but there was no way he could get there in time. Jason had his slingshot out and fumbled in his pocket for a rock. The large spider was just over Squire Josh, when suddenly, a rock bounced off the spider's head and the spider shakily withdrew, up into the large oak tree.

Sir George cut fiercely into the web with his rabbit buck teeth. Squire Josh had no more than wiggled free, when two more webs floated down, just missing them both. They dashed, zigzagging, through the woods, just out of reach of dozens of more webs dropping from the trees.

"Stop," yelled King William, "I am King William, I order you to stop."

It had no effect on the spiders, they continued to pursue. Sir George and Squire Josh had now reached King William, Tracey and Jason. When they turned to look, hundreds of spiders were now coming down out of the trees.

"Our only chance is along the shore," yelled King William. As he began to run, Tracey and Jason held tightly to King William's hair. They ran as fast as they could down the beach, but they could see that their escape was being cut off by more spiders. It was still their only hope. If they went into the cold water, the spiders would keep them trapped, either until they drowned or until they came out again. They would have to charge into the spiders and try to fight their way through, even though King William knew it was hopeless. They would soon be tangled in dozens of webs that would be thrown over them. They were only about 200 feet from the spiders on the beach now. The spiders were pursuing from behind and closing in on the sides. One of the spiders up ahead went down, a rock bouncing off his head. Then another spider went down, and another, and another. The spiders were being pelted with rocks. The spiders quickly withdrew from the beach and back to the safety of the oak trees. Dozens of spiders lay on the beach. King William, with Tracey and Jason holding tightly to his back and Sir George and Squire Josh running next to him, ran through the motionless bodies of the spiders and down the beach, to safety. King William didn't stop running until they were past the lake and at the edge of the Endless Desert. The spiders would never pursue them here. They sat panting, trying to catch their breath.

"The evil one," said King William, stopping a moment to catch his breath, "must have taken over the spiders too. We no longer know who we can trust."

"Jason," said Squire Josh, "you saved my life with your slingshot. Thank you."

"I didn't shoot any rocks," replied Jason. "I tried to, but the only rock I had was Steve."

"Well," said Sir George, with astonishment, "then where did all those rocks come from?"

"I don't know," said Jason, "but it wasn't me."

They all sat quietly for a few moments, looking at each other in amazement.

"It seems," said King William, "that we have a mysterious friend."

CHAPTER 10

▼

(THE ENDLESS DESERT)

They found some shade at the edge of the desert and rested. Late in the afternoon, when the heat began to let up, they started into the Endless Desert. Tracey and Jason had brought large leaves that they had found, which they would use for hats. They tied the leaves over their heads with vines. They also tied a large leaf over King William's head and one on the back of Squire Josh. From the top of King William's back, Squire Josh looked like nothing but a big leaf going across the desert. Sir George refused to have a big leaf tied on him but finally agreed to a smaller leaf, just big enough to shade his head. Tracey cut holes in the leaf so Sir George's ears would fit through.

It was still hot and they were soon thirsty. They didn't drink right away because they all knew they had to conserve water until they got to Crystal Springs.

"When you can almost see the other side of the desert from the mountains," asked Jason, "why do they call it the Endless Desert?"

"Because," answered Sir George, "once you start across the desert, it seems like it goes on forever, it seems endless."

"It doesn't seem so bad to me," said Jason.

"Tell me that in six days, when we reach the other side of the desert," said Sir George, "if we reach the other side at all."

They traveled until after sunset and made camp just before dark set in. They had collected some dry wood to make a camp fire. All of them drank the water sparingly and ate some of the berries they had brought along.

"We will have to get an early start in the morning," said King William, "to miss as much of the desert heat as possible."

In the morning, at first light, they were off again. They had now finished two of the gourds of water and half a gourd of berries, but kept the empty gourds to be refilled at Crystal Springs. Sir George and Squire Josh had collected and bundled two piles of dry wood to take along. One pile was stacked in front of Tracey and the other in front of Jason, just high enough so both of them could still see.

"Why are we taking wood along?" asked Tracey.

"Yeah," said Jason. "Why don't we just collect more when we stop again?"

"Tonight, when we stop again," said Sir George, "we will be in an area where almost nothing grows."

They traveled until late in the morning. The desert had become an oven and the sand almost too hot to walk on.

"We must find shade from the sun and conserve our energy," said King William.

The only thing they could find was a small ravine, where one of the walls provided some shade, until the sun was directly overhead. As the sun moved a little farther, they had shade from the other wall. They felt like they were being cooked in an oven. All of them drank only sips of water from time to time. It was later in the afternoon when they started again. They could travel only a few hours or so before they would have to stop and make camp. They were now in the area that Sir George had told them about, where almost nothing grew. It was sand and rock as far as they could see. The searing heat of the desert started to let up as the sun got lower. Just before sunset, something scurried across the sand, off to their right.

"Did you see that, Your Majesty?" asked Sir George.

"Yes," replied King William.

"See what?" asked Jason, looking around.

"Something ran across the sand, over there", said Tracey, her eyes wide.

Then, something else ran across the sand to their left and disappeared into the rocks. Tracey and Jason's head snapped in that direction.

"What are those things?" asked Tracey, a little nervous.

"They're scorpions," answered King William, "but don't worry."

"How many of them are there?" asked Jason, looking from side to side.

"Lots of them," replied King William. "That's why we brought the wood. They come out at sunset and leave just before day break."

They soon came to the crest of a small hill that sloped down on all sides.

"We'll take some of the wood and build a circle around us," said King William, "and pile the rest in the middle."

When they had finished, the sun was just setting over the horizon. Farther down the hill, they could see dozens of scorpions scurrying around. Some of the scorpions were starting to move up the hill toward them.

"Light the wood," said King William calmly.

Finally the wood was fully in flames, and it was none too soon. Dozens of scorpions scurried around the fire, looking for a way in, and hundreds more were coming up the hill.

"You never said anything about scorpions," said Tracey, as she quickly looked from side to side.

"I didn't want to worry you and Jason unnecessarily," said King William. "This is just something we have to pass through to get across the desert. The fire will keep them out."

"What about tomorrow night?" asked Jason, "we won't have anymore wood." Jason was holding his little club out in front of him with both hands, turning from side to side, ready to whack any scorpion that might get through.

"We have enough wood to tend the fire tonight," said Sir George, "and tomorrow we will be out of the scorpions' domain."

The desert was dark now. As the scorpions moved around the flickering fire, it was almost like a hypnotic dance to some music that only they could hear. Their eyes glowed red in the fire light and their tails moved up and down in rhythm. Every once in a while, one of them would try to charge through and died in the fire.

They took turns sleeping while two of them tended the fire. When the fire got low in one spot, they added wood. This went on most of the night, as hundreds of scorpions moved around, looking for their chance. It was Jason and Sir George's turn to tend the fire. It wouldn't be long until daybreak, but the wood was getting low. The fire was getting low in several places and the scorpions were moving in closer. Jason and Sir George put the last four pieces of wood where the fire was getting the lowest. On the horizon, the sky was starting to get light. The fire was burning low all around them and in one spot; it flickered from hot embers only. Jason and Sir George looked desperately for something to burn.

"Throw your club in the fire," yelled Sir George.

"No," yelled Jason, then, quickly grabbing Sir George's knife from him; ran over to King William and cut a large chunk of hair off King William's tail. Everyone was awake now, especially King William.

Jason ran over and threw the hair on the hot flickering embers. Just then, a scorpion jumped over the top. Sir George, using his strong hind legs, turned and kicked the scorpion back to the other side. Another scorpion came over the top and Jason whacked it like a baseball, sending him back. The scorpions were coming over too fast now and some got through, keeping King William, Tracey and Squire Josh busy. Then one jumped over, heading straight for Sir George's head.

Jason, with a mighty whack of his club, hit the scorpion, but in the process, hit Sir George squarely on the forehead, sending him for a loop. Just then, the hair on the embers burst into flames, stopping any more scorpions from coming through.

Daybreak had come, and the scorpions quickly began to withdraw into the shade of the rocks for the day.

"That was a close one," said Squire Josh.

They all sat for a minute, watching the scorpions disappear into the desert. Sir George was a little wobbly and there was a large lump forming on his forehead.

"I'm sorry, Sir George," apologized Jason, "I didn't mean to hit you on the head. I thought that scorpion was going to get you."

Sir George looked at Jason bleary-eyed and said, "Huh?"

Jason couldn't help but chuckle.

"Jason," glared Tracey, "it isn't funny. You just hit Sir George on the head with your club. What are you laughing about?"

"I was just thinking," chuckled Jason, "it looks like Sir George might be turning into a unicorn."

Tracey looked at Sir George. The lump on his head which was quite large now looked like the start of a horn on his forehead.

Sir George, still dazed and mouth open looked at Tracey, smiled and said, "Huh?" Tracey felt sorry for Sir George, but that did it. Tracey, King William and Squire Josh all started laughing.

They had barely survived the scorpions and were now packed and ready to go. Jason offered Sir George his spot on

King William's back, but Sir George declined, saying he was fine. The first half hour though, Sir George did a kind of zig-zag once in a while as he hopped next to King William.

The leaves they had brought for hats had dried out, but still provided some shade. By mid-morning, they found shade and again stopped to rest through the hottest part of the day. They all lay in the shade almost motionless, occasionally sipping water, eating berries and trying to conserve energy. They had now gone through almost four gourds of water and were well into the second gourd of berries. By the time they started out again, in late afternoon, they had four gourds of water left and a half a gourd of berries.

Again, they traveled until just after sunset and stopped to camp. There was dry brush again, so they built a fire. Tomorrow, by late morning, they would be at Crystal Springs. They treated themselves to an entire gourd of water that night and finished off the berries. They were in no danger here and spirits were high as they lay down to sleep.

In the morning, they awoke at daybreak. They shared another half a gourd of water between them and loaded up.

"Crystal Springs is about four hours in that direction," said King William, pointing his nose.

"What's it like?" asked Tracey, as they started off.

"You'll like it," said King William. "It's an oasis in the desert. There are cool shade trees, berry bushes and a crystal clear pool of water."

It became hot quickly, but it didn't bother any of them much. Jason even tried to sing again, but they quickly shut him up. They were not far from Crystal Springs as they finished off the other half gourd of water. They had done very well on the water. They would still have two gourds left when they reached Crystal Springs.

"Just over the next rise," said King William, "we'll be able to see Crystal Springs in the distance."

They were all very happy as they approached the top of the rise. There, in the distance, was Crystal Springs. King William stopped and gave a gasp of disbelief. Something was wrong. Instead of green trees waving softly in the desert breeze, everything was brown, like the desert sand.

It took them about another hour to get there. The trees and berry bushes were dead and brown. Next to the pool of water were several skeletons of animals that had tried to drink there.

King William shook his head in disbelief. "The evil one has poisoned the water. I should have suspected this."

"What are we going to do now?" asked Tracey, in a concerned voice.

King William, in an attempt to raise their fallen spirits, said in a very positive voice, "We will rest in the shade of these dead trees and continue on this afternoon. We still have two gourds of water. If we are careful, that will be enough."

Jason picked up, "Yeah, we can do it. That Evil One can't stop us. We're the Fearsome Fivesome."

"This is just one more reason to kick butt!" said Tracey angrily.

"Right," said Squire Josh, "we'll show the Evil One not to mess with us."

They all looked at Sir George, who was at a temporary loss for words. Finally he said, "Well—the evil one has sure got me hopping mad."

They all sat there for a second and burst into laughter, even Sir George. King William had tried to lift their spirits and it turned out, they had lifted his.

Chapter 11

▼

(ACROSS THE DESERT)

In the afternoon, they all took a sip of water and started off again. Each was determined not to let the desert or the Evil One get the best of them. The sun seemed hotter than it had ever been and the desert stretched on and on. Jason now knew why they called it the Endless Desert.

It was late in the afternoon when Tracey noticed something above them.

"Look at that," said Tracey, "above us."

King William stopped, "Buzzards," he said, "they think they're going to get a meal."

They continued on and stopped at dusk. The buzzards had disappeared. They made a campfire and as they had done every two hours, each took a sip of water. They laid down, exhausted, and slept.

Tracey woke up to the sound of pecking and water running on the ground. She sat up and screamed, "Get out of here!"

They were all awake now, as two buzzards flew away. The buzzards had pecked holes in the two gourds that held the water. The last of their water disappeared quickly into the dry desert sand. It was dawn as they all stood looking at the broken, empty gourds.

"Even the buzzards, it seems." said King William, "are controlled by the Evil One. We must go on. We will take only two of the other empty gourds with us, in case we find water."

They left, hungry and thirsty with still more than two days to travel across the desert. Between them and the Dark Forest there were no springs and no rivers. There weren't even any cactus that grew in this desert, that they could squeeze water out of. King William knew it was impossible to make it without water. He suspected that Tracey and Jason also knew, but if they didn't, he wasn't going to tell them.

They stopped again at mid-morning and rested in the shade. When afternoon came, they had all they could do to get up and continue on. They moved slowly across the desert. Each step was an effort. At dusk, they built a camp fire and lay down. They fell to sleep with their stomachs aching and their lips parched and sore.

Tracey heard the sound of flapping wings and pushed herself up on one elbow. It was dawn and the buzzards were back. Still lying down, she picked up a rock and threw it at them. From where he lay, Jason nailed a couple of them with his slingshot. The buzzards left, but Tracey knew they would be back. Maybe the buzzards would get their meal after all.

Even King William's great strength had left him. He was only able to lift his head and watch. Sir George and Squire Josh didn't even move. Tracey didn't know if they were alive or dead. Jason was already sleeping again as Tracey laid her head down and closed her eyes, maybe for the last time.

Tracey heard the sound of flapping wings again, but she was too tired and too weak to do anything. There was a pecking on her cheek. She still didn't move. Again, there was a pecking on her cheek, but it was a gentle pecking. Tracey turned her head and half opened her eyes. There, stood a beautiful white dove and next to Tracey's head was a fat, juicy plum. With all of her strength, Tracey pushed herself up on one elbow and bit into the juicy plum. She could almost feel the strength and energy flowing into her body. There were several other doves, all carrying plums. Jason was now half up, eating one of the plums, as was King William. Sir George and Squire Josh lay motionless. Tracey struggled over to Sir George. She took a plum, picked up the little rabbit's head and squeezed plum juice into his mouth.

"Sir George," said Tracey, her voice scratchy and tears in her eyes, "please don't die."

One of the beautiful doves came over. "Did you say Sir George? —is this Sir George?"

Tracey was startled at the dove talking, but was too weak and too sad to react. "Yes," said Tracey, a tear running down her cheek, "this is the brave and wonderful Sir George."

Just then the little rabbit's tongue started to move, taking in the juices from the plum. Sir George's eyes half opened. The beautiful white dove moved closer and with a tear in her eye said, "Sir George, it's me, your wife, Lady Jane."

Sir George's eyes opened wide and in a scratchy voice said, "Oh! my beautiful Lady Jane. Have I died? Am I in Heaven?"

"No," said Lady Jane, "you haven't died, but I think we're both in Heaven." A tear of joy ran off her beak.

Tracey struggled over to Squire Josh. She held the little dog's head and squeezed plum juice into his mouth, but Squire Josh didn't move. The tears ran down Tracey's face because she knew he was dead. She leaned over and kissed him on the head and laid his head down. Tracey swore she would kill the Evil One herself. Suddenly, Squire Josh's tongue moved a little. Tracey quickly squeezed more plum juice into his mouth and the little dog began to lap it up as fast as she squeezed. Tracey was now laughing and crying at the same time, but the tears were tears of happiness.

More doves flew in carrying plums and other small fruits. They came from the side of the desert near the dark forest. At mid-morning, the heat had become too much for even the doves, so they stayed and told stories, waiting for the hottest part of the day to pass.

The Evil One had turned all of King William's loyal subjects into various kinds of animals. All of the women of the castle, except one, were turned into white doves, who were constantly being hunted by the evil one's hawks. The doves were all overwhelmed with joy, of course, that King William was still alive. When Jason produced Steve, the Rock, the doves flocked all over him, cooing with pleasure. Jason thought it was fun for awhile, but that didn't last long and he shooed them away. However, one little dove continued to follow him around wherever he went.

Late in the afternoon, the doves began bringing more fruit. King William thought it would be better if they stayed where they were until morning, eating fruit, resting and regaining their strength.

That evening, around the camp fire, a mystery was solved.

Lady Jane explained, as she sat near Sir George, "We saw you at Spider Lake, but didn't know who you were. We knew that the Evil One had taken control of the spiders, so when we saw the spiders throw a web over Squire Josh; we knew that you must be one of us. We've become very accurate with rocks from quite high up. The first rock we used on the spider who was after Squire Josh, the rest of the rocks we used on the spiders on the beach, who were trying to block your escape. Pargon and the hawks have been very active, hunting us, but we've tried to protect you ever since."

"Thank you," said King William. "We owe you our lives for the second time. There are still many dangers ahead", said Lady Jane. "But, now that we know you are alive, and you have the Rock, we are all filled with great hope and joy."

"It is loss of hope," said Sir George, "that the Evil One thrives on."

King William looked at Lady Jane and the rest of the doves. "I know that bringing us this fruit has been very dangerous for you. Each time you fly, you risk being killed by the hawks. You have brought us enough fruit to last us across the desert. It will be two days before we enter the Dark Forest, another two days through the Dark Forest and another day to Howling Rocks. Tomorrow, I want you to fly back to the safety of the woods, on the other side of the Dark Forest. Spread the word, to all of us who are left, to meet at Howling Rocks in six days".

"Your Majesty," said Lady Jane, "we will bring everyone we can to Howling Rocks."

"I know," said King William, "that you can fly over the Dark Forest, but for a dove to actually go into the Dark Forest would be almost certain death. I am ordering that none of you enter the Dark Forest to check on us, under any circumstances. Do you understand?"

"Yes, Your Majesty," all of the doves replied.

They built a large camp fire and rested for the night. Squire Josh, who was now Tracey's constant companion, was near Tracey, to guard her. Sir George and Lady Jane were together and the little dove that Tracey had found out was named Jill, was not far from Jason. The rest of the doves were scattered around King William.

In the morning, they all said their good-byes and the doves flew off to the woods, on the other side of the Dark Forest, where they would be much safer.

King William had Tracey and Jason on his back, with two gourds of fruit, one on each side of him tied together with a vine. The five of them, or seven, if you count L'il Lucas and Hombre, were off on the last part of their journey across the desert.

They traveled until mid-morning. Again, they rested during the hottest part of the day and traveled until dusk, when they set up camp. That night, their spirits were high as they ate lots of fruit and watched the camp fire. They knew that late tomorrow morning, they would be near the Dark Forest. There would be lots of berries to eat and cool water to drink. They also knew that they were not alone. There were many others ready to join them and help them. Tracey and Jason talked about Mom and Dad and how much they missed home. When they laid down to sleep that night, with L'il Lucas and Hombre, Tracey and Jason slept better than they had since they came to the Land of Cigam.

CHAPTER 12

▼

(BAT CAVE)

Not long after they left camp, they could see the green forest in the distance. Gradually, there appeared more vegetation in the desert.

King Billy," said Jason, in one of his jovial moods, "I want you to know that Tracey and I really appreciate the ride."

"Why Jason," laughed King William, "all that sun must have affected your brain. You're actually thanking me for something."

"Well," said Jason laughing, "just don't get too used to it."

"Since we're giving out thanks," smiled King William, "I would like to thank you for figuring out a way to get us across the bridge at the Bottomless Canyon and also for stopping the scorpions. However, if you need to save us in the future, would you try to figure out a way that doesn't involve my tail?" Everybody started laughing, especially King William.

As the forest got closer, the little clusters of weeds turned into small scrubs. The small scrubs turned into bushes and the bushes into trees. The weather had cooled to where it was now comfortable and the shade from the trees was refreshing to Tracey and Jason's sunburned bodies. They came to a cool stream and lots of juicy berry bushes and fruit trees. They had made it through what Jason now referred to as The Endless Desert.

On the horizon, they could see the cloud-covered mountains where the Evil One dwelled. Tracey and Jason were sitting on a rock near a stream, enjoying the cool weather. Squire Josh jumped up on the rock next to Tracey.

Tracey smiled at Squire Josh and asked, "Lady Jane said that the Evil One had turned all the ladies of the castle into doves except one. What did she mean?"

Squire Josh looked surprised. He looked around to see if anyone was close. "You mean you really don't know?" he asked.

"No," said Tracey.

"Uh, uh," said Jason, shaking his head.

Squire Josh looked around again and said, "We never talk about it in front of the King. He had a beautiful wife, Queen Genevive. She was the most beautiful woman in the whole kingdom. When the Evil One crept into our lives and took over, the dark power was concentrated through her. She is no longer beautiful and looks as horrible as the evil that emanates through her.

"You mean the Evil One is a woman?" asked Jason.

"No," answered Squire Josh, "Evil is neither a man nor a woman, it is just using the Queen. Evil is nothing but evil."

"Wow," said Tracey in astonishment, "the King never said anything, he must be very sad."

"He is," said Squire Josh sadly, "and he fears that he will not be able to drive the Evil One out without killing his Queen."

They set up camp near the stream, deciding to leave early in the morning. They would cover as much ground as possible through the Dark Forest the first day.

It was good to be in cooler weather again and the sound of running water was music to their ears. There were still many dangers that lay ahead, but they would not go thirsty again.

It seemed to Tracey that she had no more than closed her eyes and it was time to get up. Jason didn't want to get up, but finally struggled to his feet. After they had eaten, Tracey and Jason climbed on King William's back and started down the path leading to the Dark Forest.

"It is very important," said King William, "that you stay close to me at all times. The paths through the forest can be very tricky and dangerous."

Sir George had showed Tracey and Jason how to make two torches, which they carried across King William's back.

"When does the forest get dark enough for the torches?" asked Jason.

"Oh, the forest doesn't get that dark," said Sir George, hopping along next to them. "Except at night, of course, and we'll build a fire at night."

"Wait a minute," said Tracey, concerned, "I have a feeling that there is something you haven't told us. Exactly what are the torches for?"

"The torches are for the cave," answered Sir George.

"All right," said Jason excitedly, "a cave."

Tracey looked concerned. "Where is this cave?" she asked.

"It's only about an hour from here," answered Sir George.

Tracey didn't like what she was hearing. "Well— how big is the cave?"

"It only takes about 45 minutes to get through the cave," said Sir George.

Jason was still excited. "Tray, this is going to be neat, going through a cave."

Tracey ignored Jason. "Why didn't you tell us about it?" asked Tracey, her face a little red with anger.

"It was my decision," said King William, "we didn't want to worry you unnecessarily."

"I am worried," said Tracey, "does the cave have a name?"

No one said anything.

Tracey was irritated. "Well——it must have a name."

"It's called Bat Cave," said King William.

"Oh great!!" said Tracey, I don't like rats, I don't like spiders, I don't like scorpions and I hate bats. Now we're going through Bat Cave. Isn't there some way to go around?"

"There is," said King William, "but, it would take days and we don't have the time. The bats won't bother us as long as we have the torches and don't make too much noise."

Jason did his Dracula impression. "Von't youuu step intoo my caaaave for a little bite?"

Tracey was mad now. "Jason—just shut up."

Jason laughed, "Lighten up Tray, it'll be fun." Then he went back to his Dracula impression. "Truuust me my dear, youuu'll have a bloooody good time." Then he began laughing again.

King William, Sir George and Squire Josh didn't quite know what Jason was doing, but they thought it was funny.

So, while Tracey sat red faced and angry, the others laughed.

As they moved deeper into the forest, it became thicker and darker. The forest seemed to close in on them as the huge trees formed a canopy above them. Occasionally, a ray of sunlight would sneak through the thick foliage to light their way. When they got close to the cave, the forest opened up for them like a door—— daring them to enter Bat Cave.

The mouth of the cave was large, set in the shear rock face of a ridge that stretched in both directions. Vines grew over most of the face, but they weren't strong enough to support much weight. Even if they could hold the weight, King William, Sir George and Squire Josh wouldn't be able to climb them.

"We'll light only one torch at a time," said King William. "When the first torch burns low, we'll light the second torch. Make as little noise as possible. The less noise we make, the less we'll disturb the bats."

The torch Tracey was holding was lit first. As they moved slowly into the cave, Tracey had the feeling they were entering the mouth of some giant creature that would swallow them forever.

It wasn't long before the cave was pitch black and only the dancing flame from the little torch lit the narrow path they were following. The light flickered off the walls and reflected off hundreds of beady little eyes, high on the top of the cave. From time to time, there would be a few screeches and the fluttering of wings among the bats, but it would quickly settle down. They moved as quietly as possible along the narrow path.

When Tracey's torch burned low, she lit the one Jason was holding and dropped hers on the ground, before it burned her hand.

They were well past half way. The cave had changed. There was a deep gully that ran along the right side of them now and they could hear the sound of dripping and running water. The cave was now very cold and Tracey could hardly wait to get out.

Finally, they saw a light at the end of the tunnel. Jason was so happy, he let out a whoop. Pandemonium broke out in the cave. The yell had disturbed thousands of bats and they swarmed all over the cave. The bats were screeching and flapping all around them. Jason ducked down, but as he did, he dropped the torch and it rolled down into the gully. There was a hissing sound as the torch hit the water. The cave went black, except for the little light from the end of the tunnel, which barely lit their way.

"Hang on," yelled King William, as he began running for the light at the end of the cave. With each stride it got lighter and with each stride there were fewer bats. Finally, they burst out of the cave and into the light.

They stopped, a little way out of the cave, trying to catch their breath. Tracey was so relieved at being out of the cave she was laughing, while trying to catch her breath at the same time.

"Jason—you idiot," laughed Tracey, "I hope you had fun."

Jason didn't answer. Tracey turned around, still laughing. Jason sat frozen, his eyes wide with fright. On his shoulder sat a rather large black bat. The bat may have been more frightened than Jason at everything that was going on, and quickly flew off and back into the cave. Everybody, except Jason of course, was laughing so hard, they were laying on the ground. Jason sat on a nearby rock, red-faced and embarrassed.

They were still chuckling as they started off again, into the Dark Forest.

Tracey now did her impression of Dracula. "Jasooon, vould youu step into my caaave for a little bite?"

Everybody, except Jason, started laughing again, but kept on going. Jason sat on the back of King William, arms crossed and red-faced.

CHAPTER 13

▼

(THE DARK FOREST)

The forest quickly closed in on them, again forming a canopy over their heads. Before the sun had even set over the horizon, it was dark enough in the forest to set up camp for the night. The wood in the forest was so moist they had to take Sir George's knife and shave some dry wood off Jason's club to start a fire. It took awhile, but they finally got a fire started and gathered enough wood for the night.

Two springs bubbled nearby, so they had plenty of fresh water. There was also plenty to eat, but Sir George had to show them which fruits they could eat and which ones they couldn't.

"It's very important that you ask me before you eat anything here in the Dark Forest," said Sir George. "Some of these fruits are not good for you and some of them are actually poisonous. You can't always tell by the look or the smell."

"Jason," said Tracey, a little irritated, "you aren't paying attention."

"Yes I am," said Jason, munching down on one of the fruits Sir George said he could eat.

Many strange sounds came out of the forest at night. There was clicking and clacking, creaking and croaking, bird screams, rustling in the brush near the camp and howling in the distance. Sometimes they could see the reflection of light against eyes that were peering in at them.

"The animals of the forest," said King William, "are afraid of fire. They won't bother us as long as we keep the fire burning and this fire will burn all night."

"When we're traveling through the forest," said Tracey, "how do you know which way to go?"

King William smiled, "We've been through here so many times, even though the forest changes, the people that live here have a sense for it. We just know. But, you have to be very careful. The forest can be very tricky. There are paths everywhere. One wrong turn and you can be lost—Or worse yet, end up in the Death Swamp."

"What's the Death Swamp?" asked Jason.

"The Death Swamp," said King William "is just what it sounds like. It is said that there are creatures there that———. Well, — enough of that. It is a swamp that many people have gone into, but no one has ever come out of."

They talked a little while longer, and then piled a little more wood on the fire to make sure it would last all night. It made Tracey and Jason nervous to go to sleep in the forest, but they were so tired, it didn't take long.

Jason was the first one to wake up. It was just starting to get light in the forest. The fire was still burning, just as King William said it would. Jason rubbed his eyes and felt around for his slingshot. Hombre was there, but where was his slingshot? Jason sat there for a moment thinking. He remembered, he must have laid it down by the spring yesterday, when he was getting a drink. "Hombre," he whispered, "I'll be right back."

Jason ran down the path to the spring. There it was, laying on a rock. He picked it up and examined it. "Good as new," he said, stuffing it in his back pocket. Jason turned around to go back. He hadn't noticed the other two paths on his way to the spring. He was sure he had taken the center one and started back to camp. After walking for awhile, he realized he should have already been back to the camp.

"It must have been one of the other paths," he muttered, "I better go back to the spring." But, there were other paths, angling right and left. He went up one path and down another. He became frightened and started running down the paths, desperately searching for the right one.

"Can anybody hear me?" he yelled. But the dense forest swallowed up the sound like a giant sponge.

They had all been awake at the camp for several minutes before they realized Jason was gone. Tracey saw Hombre lying on the ground next to where Jason had been sleeping.

"Jason," she called, but there was no answer. "We've got to find him," she told King William, anxiously. Tracey started down one of the paths, but King William stopped her.

"Tracey," said King William, "we don't need two of you lost. Let me send out Sir George and Squire Josh. If Jason is nearby, they will find him. You and I will stay here in case Jason comes back."

For the next hour King William sat, watching Tracey pace back and forth. Every so often, she would call her brother's name into the woods, hoping for a reply. Finally, Sir George and Squire Josh came back. Tracey watched anxiously. Without a word, Sir George looked at King William and shook his head from side to side.

"But we can't just leave him," said Tracey pleadingly. "We have to stay here, we have to find him."

"Tracey," said King William sadly, "we can't stay any longer. We have to go. Many lives depend on us and we are already behind schedule."

"You can't go anyway," said Tracey, trying to figure out some argument to make them stay, "he has Steve, — he has the Magic Rock."

"I know," said King William, understanding her sorrow, "But, we will have to face the Evil One, whether we have the Rock or not. We will have to face the Evil One on our own."

"You go ahead," said Tracey, "I'll wait here for Jason." Tracey went over and sat down on a rock.

King William went over and sat down next to Tracey. "Tracey," he said softly, "in three days we are going to battle the Evil One. If we lose, we are all lost anyway. If we win, I promise you, I will send my entire Kingdom to find your brother. In the meantime, we need your help. Come with us."

As they left, Tracey looked back, with tears in her eyes. She had never ridden King William without Jason. She had L'il

Lucas and Hombre with her, but Tracey had never felt so alone.

CHAPTER 14

▼

(THE DEATH SWAMP)

Jason wandered for hours, trying to find a way out. There were paths everywhere, just as King William had said. A path would start out in one direction and then twist and turn in another direction. Jason became excited when it started getting lighter and the forest wasn't as dense. He had found his way out of the Dark Forest, he thought. Now it wouldn't be hard to find Tracey and the rest of them.

"It must have rained," he thought. "There's a puddle over there." A little while later he noticed another puddle. Jason took out his slingshot and started checking it over, as he walked. He didn't know how long he had been walking, when he heard a bubbling sound. Jason looked around him and was almost completely surrounded by green murky water. Only the paths that led everywhere were above the slime. Dead trees were lying on their sides, half sticking out of the water. The trees that were still standing were leafless and looked like great skeletons standing in the gray mist. He had been so busy working on his slingshot that he hadn't noticed all the strange sounds which now surrounded him. King William's words rang in his ears. "The Death Swamp is a place that many people have gone into, but no one has ever come out of." And what was it King William was going to tell them about the strange creatures in the swamp before he changed his mind? A shiver of fear went through Jason's body, because he knew he had wandered into the Death Swamp.

It was getting dark and a fog was starting to form over the murky water. Jason knew he had to find a safe place to spend the night. He walked a little longer and finally spotted a huge dead tree standing not far from the path. It looked strong enough to hold him. Jason made his way across a half-submerged log and climbed as high as he thought he safely could. He wedged himself in one of the crotches of the tree and waited.

It soon became dark and the fog closed in around him. Strange sounds echoed through the fog, some he thought were too close for comfort. He hugged against the tree, almost as if he were trying to become a part of the tree—disappear into it, so he wouldn't be noticed. He knew he was too scared to fall asleep tonight, but soon dozed off and slept.

It was the screech of some swamp dweller, probably a bird that woke Jason up. It was light, but the fog was too thick to see more than ten feet. He was cold and ached all over, but didn't want to move until some of the fog lifted and he could see better. He was so hungry he thought he could eat the tree.

It was mid-morning before the fog lifted enough to climb down from the tree. Jason's body was so stiff it didn't want to move. He almost fell off the log he had to cross to get back to the path. It felt good to be back on solid ground again. He was cold, hungry and thirsty as he looked around, trying to figure out which way to go. Jason made his mind up and started down a path. As he stopped for a moment, to tie his shoe, he noticed something in the dirt. There were tracks. It looked like large dog tracks. Jason's heart stopped. Wolves! They were wolf tracks! Jason looked around nervously. From now on, he must constantly be on the lookout and always have a plan of escape. He was only starting to become aware of the true dangers of the swamp. But the first thing he had to do was find something to eat.

After wandering for about an hour, Jason came to a patch of dry land—a small island in the swamp. There were fruit trees, like the ones in the Dark Forest, and a bubbling spring of clear water. He knelt beside the spring and drank. Jason felt refreshed as he sat on a rock looking at the fruit trees. He couldn't remember what Sir George had said about the fruit. The type of fruit Jason had eaten in the Dark Forest wasn't here, but there were two other kinds that Sir George had talked about. Jason smelled both kinds of fruit. One smelled bitter and the other smelled like a peach. Jason was so hungry, he had to choose. He took a little bite out of the one that smelled like a peach. It was delicious. Jason threw the bitter one away and finished eating the one he had chosen. It was juicy and just one completely satisfied his hunger.

Now, to try to figure out a way out of here, he took another one of the fruits for later and started down the new path he had chosen. Jason felt much more confident, now that he had survived a night in the swamp and found something to eat. It had only been about 20 minutes since Jason ate, when he tripped on a root in the path. He got up feeling a little dizzy. He walked down the path a little ways and bumped a tree with his shoulder, almost knocking himself down. He staggered back, stepping off the path and falling into the slimy green water. As he stood up in the water, something slithered by him. Jason managed to pull himself up on the path, where he collapsed.

Everything seemed like a dream, as if it were a million miles away. He heard what sounded like wolves, howling in the distance. The howling kept getting closer until he could almost hear their growls and their footsteps on the path. There was a roar that shook the ground like an explosion and the wolves were gone. Something had a hold of him, something was moving him and then there was nothing.

Jill, the little dove knew she was flying to almost certain death. But, if Jason were still alive, she knew, she had to find him and help him. She had several close calls in the Dark Forest and was now flying into the Death Swamp. The fog had lifted, which made it easier for her to see. But, it also made it easier for her enemies to see her. Jill had been flying in the Death Swamp for about a half an hour, when a hawk spotted her. Jill flew close to the swamp, dodging in and out of the dead trees. The hawk was after her. If she didn't find something very quickly, she knew she was dead. There——there was a large cave in the side of the hill. There were dangers in the cave, but she had no choice. Jill flew into the cave. The hawk, for some reason, didn't follow.

The cave was surprisingly warm. She cautiously walked back into the cave. She couldn't believe it. There by a fire, lay Jason. She quickly flew over next to him.

"Jason, can you hear me?" She was afraid he was dead.

Jason stirred. Twice he tried to push himself up on one elbow and twice he failed. He was very weak, but the third time, he made it. Jason's eyes were blurred, but began to clear a little. "Jill," is that you?" He had trouble speaking.

"Yes," she answered. "Jason, what's the matter with you?"

"I think," said Jason, "I ate something I shouldn't have. How did you get me here?"

"Jason," said Jill, "I didn't bring you here, I just now found you here."

"Where are the others?" asked Jason.

"They couldn't wait any longer," said Jill. "They're on their way to Howling Rocks. Jason, you have the Magic Rock. They need the Magic Rock."

There was a noise at the entrance to the cave. Something huge was coming into the cave. When Jason and Jill, saw what it was, they knew they were dead.

▼

CHAPTER 15

(THE HOWLING ROCKS)

It was now late afternoon and soon King William and his little band would be out of the Dark Forest. The dense forest that surrounded them would thin out to a peaceful wooded area, where they could make camp for the night. Suddenly, there was a rustling in the bushes up ahead and a young boy about 12 jumped onto the path in front of them, sword in hand.

"Halt," he demanded, "who goes there?"

King William came to a stop. "It is I, King William, rightful ruler of all this land. I am accompanied by Sir George, Squire Josh and Maid Tracey."

The young boy stuck the point of his sword in the path and knelt. "Your Majesty," he said, "if you are going to fight the Evil One, then my sword is yours to command."

"What is your name, lad?" asked King William.

"Your Majesty," he answered angrily, "my name is Tony and I am not a boy, I am a warrior. My father was a great warrior, from a distant land, who taught me well. My father died fighting the Evil One and I am here for vengeance. I will fight bravely by your side or I will fight alone, the choice is yours."

"Very well warrior Tony," said King William, "we bid you welcome. Rise and join us."

Tony traveled with them the rest of the way through the Dark Forest. He talked nonstop, telling them of his life and how his father had trained him to be a great warrior until the Evil One had killed his father, by trickery. He told how he had found out about King William from the doves, who were rousing everyone they could to fight.

They were in the woods now, just outside the Dark Forest. It was getting dark and King William ordered camp to be set up. Tony continued to talk, non-stop, throughout the whole evening.

When Tracey laid down to sleep, she wondered about Jason and if he were safe. She also wondered if they would ever see Mom and Dad again. She missed her family so much. As Tracey drifted off to sleep, Tony was still by the camp fire, talking.

Tracey was awakened by a soft pecking on her cheek. She sat up and rubbed her eyes.

"Good morning Tracey," came the soft voice of Lady Jane. She and Sir George were laughing softly. "Did you have a good sleep?" she asked.

The sun was over the horizon. "Oh my gosh, did I oversleep?" asked Tracey anxiously.

"We've been up since dawn," said Sir George.

"But you were sleeping so soundly," added Lady Jane, "we thought we would let you sleep a little longer."

Suddenly, Tracey was wide awake. "Has anyone heard anything about my brother?" she asked anxiously.

"I'm sorry," said Lady Jane, "no one knows anything. We are all hoping for the best."

Tracey got up and they went over to where King William sat with Squire Josh and dozens of doves. Squire Josh immediately got up and went over to sit next to Tracey.

Tracey looked around. "Where's Tony?" she asked.

King William answered, "I asked Tony to go to the village near the castle and raise as many villagers as he could, to fight with us. Lady Jane has informed me that we are having trouble getting the villagers to join us. It seems that they are much too afraid. I thought that if anyone could raise their spirits and talk them into fighting, Tony could." Then King William mumbled to himself, "I've never seen anyone that could talk as much as that young man."

A dove landed next to Lady Jane and whispered in her ear.

"Is anything wrong Lady Jane?" asked King William.

"Your Majesty," said Lady Jane, "I'm afraid the little dove named Jill is gone. She must have overheard us talking about Jason. We think she has gone to the Dark Forest or the Death Swamp to find him."

King William lowered his head. "The doves have so many enemies there that her fate is almost certainly sealed," he said.

"Your Majesty, we still have much work to do," said Lady Jane.

"And we," said King William, "still have a long way to travel."

The doves said their good-byes and left. Tracey quickly ate, drank some water and they were off———-off to Howling Rocks.

It wasn't long before they started into the foothills at the base of the mountains. The dark clouds that hung over the mountains soon blotted out the sun. King William took every back trail he knew, to keep them from being detected. It was late that afternoon when they reached Howling Rocks, not far from the castle. Tracey soon found out why they called this place Howling Rocks. Everywhere, there were tall, strange rock formations and when the wind blew through the rocks; they made a mournful howling sound.

Tracey climbed up on the rocks to where she could see. Not far in the distance was the castle. The dark clouds, particularly over the castle, gave it a bleak and foreboding look. A large gray stone wall completely surrounded the entire castle and grounds. Heavy wooden gates led into a very large courtyard, with the castle set well back. The castle itself was made of the same gray stone as the wall, and Tracey could see that it once must have been like a castle out of a fairy tale. Now it stood like a giant tombstone, gray, cold and lifeless. A short distance away, down in the valley, was the village where King William had sent Tony.

Some of King William's army had already arrived and more were coming all the time. King William sat patiently as each one slowly filed by, identifying themselves and swearing allegiance. Of all of King William's knights, there were only ten rabbits left besides Sir George. The rest had been killed. There were several small dogs who had been squires, like Squire Josh. The castle guard had been turned into raccoons. The cooks and kitchen workers had been turned into pigs. The soldiers had been turned into sheep and the court jester had been turned into an ostrich. It seemed the Evil One had a sense of humor.

King William finally had to put a stop to the procession. It was getting late and they needed rest for the next day. King William welcomed them all and bid them good night. They couldn't risk camp fires, so they had to huddle wherever they could to keep warm. It wasn't easy trying to go to sleep with the rocks howling every time a gust of wind came through. But the events of the last two days had completely drained Tracey and like the night before, she fell asleep, thinking of her family.

When Tracey woke in the morning, many more creatures had arrived. There were now possums, squirrels, deer and more. They all knew the risk they were taking, fighting by the side of King William. It was better to fight side by side and die, than to be hunted down and killed one at a time by the followers of the Evil One. The last to arrive were the doves. Lady Jane told Tracey that there was still no word about Jason.

"Your Majesty," said Lady Jane, "young Tony tried to rouse the villagers to fight, but they were too afraid. Tony has been arrested by the Evil One's guard and taken to the castle …"

"Are there no villagers who will fight?" asked King William in amazement.

"None," replied Lady Jane.

A lookout came down from the rocks. He told King William that the gates to the castle were open. There were no guards on the walls and except for someone tied to a stake in the middle of the courtyard, the courtyard was empty.

King William turned and looked at his small army. Tracey stood next to him. "The gates to the castle are open," he said, in a clear powerful voice. "There is no doubt that it is a trap. All of you are aware of the dangers we face today. Our army is small and we do not have the Magic Rock, but some battles must be won with our hearts. If any of you want to leave now, I will not hold it against you."

No one moved. Tracey whispered in King William's ear.

King William continued. "To all of you who follow me today, I say, give me liberty or give me death."

The effect those words had on King William's little army was overwhelming. Tracey couldn't help but get a lump in her throat and a tear in her eye. Those same words had been spoken by one of her own countrymen over 200 years ago. It was a different time and a different place and still, they so moved the hearts of these people. Tracey had learned those words in school, but until now they were only words. Now, those words had meaning. If she ever got home, Tracey promised herself, she would thank her history teacher.

CHAPTER 16

▼

(THE BATTLE)

King William and his little army moved cautiously through the open gates. It was Tony who was tied to a stake in the middle of the courtyard. Tony had been gagged, but shook his head back and forth as if he was warning them. They moved forward and cut him free. Tony pulled the gag from his mouth and yelled, "It's a trap."

"So William, you have made the mistake of coming back." The icy voice came from a balcony on the castle. There, dressed in red, was the most evil looking person Tracey had ever seen.

"Yes," said King William, with authority, "I have come to claim my Kingdom and take back my lovely wife, Queen Genevive."

"Oh," said the icy voice, then posing, "do you still think she's lovely?"

"She will be lovely again, when you are dead," replied King William.

"You fool," roared the Evil One, "you don't even have the rock. The boy has it and he has been swallowed up by the Death Swamp."

A chilling fear went through Tracey's heart. Was Jason dead? She thought.

"Then we will drive you out without the Rock," said King William.

The woman on the balcony shook and grasped the rail. "William, my King," it was a different voice, soft and loving. "I love you, go back." The woman shook again and straightened up.

"See, the icy voice had returned, as smiling, she said. Your Queen still fights me, but it is useless, she grows weaker each day. Now she will see her King die."

She clapped her hands and the mighty gates to the courtyard slammed shut. Around one side of the castle came Yuk, followed by hundreds of spiders and scorpions. Around the other side of the castle came Ikar and his army of rats. Flying up and sitting all over the castle were the buzzards and circling high above the castle were the hawks. She clapped her hands again and the evil army charged forward.

King William's small little army was almost overwhelmed by the onslaught. They fought fiercely and valiantly but were no match for the evil army. Slowly, they were being pushed back toward the wall, with no place to go.

Suddenly, there was a thunderous crash and a cloud of dust as the mighty gates to the courtyard came crashing down. Through what had once been the gates, came a fire-breathing dragon. The Evil One had brought a dragon to finish them off, thought King William.

But wait, —————the dragon was clawing and snapping and breathing fire at the evil army. The dragon began to fight its way over toward King William's army, using its great tail to sweep away the enemy that tried to swarm in behind. That's when they noticed, on the back of the dragon, Jason, and on his shoulder the little dove, Jill. Tracey laughed with a tear in her eye as she waved at her smiling brother.

The tide of the battle had turned and King William's army began to push forward. Pushing the evil army back toward the castle, hundreds more rats, spiders and scorpions began to pour in from both sides of the castle. King William's army slowed and stopped. Although King William's army fought as hard as they could, they were again being pushed back.

The Evil One had called the archers to the walls and arrows rained down upon them. The dragon had been struck at least three times, but fought on. Tony, the brave little warrior, had been struck with an arrow in the leg but valiantly continued to fight, swinging his sword as he hopped back on one leg. They couldn't hold out much longer.

There was a commotion outside the walls of the castle. Suddenly, dozens of villagers came pouring through the fallen gates. They were carrying shovels, hoes, clubs, sticks and anything else that they could use for a weapon. Even above the noise of the battle, they could hear the Evil One shriek with anger.

The archers on the walls started dropping, one by one. The doves had come into the battle and were dropping rocks with deadly accuracy. Down came the hawks after the doves. The only hope the doves had of surviving was to fly into the courtyard and land among King William's army. But, they had done their job. They had taken out almost all of the deadly archers.

Once again, King William's army, with renewed strength, pushed forward. This time they pushed to within fifty feet of the castle door before they were stopped. The Evil One had waited until now to send in her wolves. The fierce packs of wolves came from both sides of the castle. King William's army could go no further.

"King William," yelled Tracey, "where is the ALTAR of light?"

"Through that window there," yelled King William, "just above the balcony where the Evil One stands."

Tracey turned and yelled at Jason. "Jason," she called, cupping her hand over her mouth to direct the sound. Jason, sitting on the dragon's back, leaned over to hear.

"Jason," she yelled again, "the window over the balcony———can you see the altar?"

Jason sat up and looked for a moment and then looked back at Tracey and nodded yes.

Tracey yelled to Jason, "The Rock," and then she acted as if she was shooting a slingshot at the window.

Jason sat looking at her for a moment and then smiled. He reached in his pocket and took out 'Steve', the Rock. He placed 'Steve' carefully in his slingshot and looked at the window. Jason pulled the slingshot back, taking careful aim. Just as he was about to let go, the rubber on his slingshot broke.

Jason quickly tried to fix his slingshot, but it was no use. The battle raged and they were starting to be pushed back again.

"Tray," yelled Jason and he threw the rock to her. It was too high for her to catch and it went over her head. As Tracey turned around, she heard a loud groan. The rock had hit King William on the hind foot and now lay on the ground. King William was limping and shaking his foot while he continued fighting.

Tracey picked up the rock and looked at Jason, shrugging her shoulders as if to say, "What am I supposed to do with this?" Jason made a motion like a softball pitcher. Tracey used to pitch softball back home and knew immediately what Jason meant.

Tracey shook her head no and yelled, "It's too far."

Jason yelled, "No it's not," and then added, "Tray, it's our only hope."

Tracey looked at the window. The rock was too heavy for the doves.

Almost no one saw the lone archer on the wall take careful aim at Tracey's heart.

Tracey took the stance of a softball pitcher and concentrated on the window.

The archer let the arrow fly, true to its course, straight for Tracey's heart.

Tracey was about to pitch the rock, when something came flying through the air in front of her. There was a yelp and it fell to the ground in front of her. Tracey looked down and saw Squire Josh lying motionless on the ground, with an arrow sticking in him. Tracey knelt down next to Squire Josh.

"No," she cried, not Squire Josh. The little dog had taken the arrow meant for her.

Tracey jumped to her feet; tears were streaming down her face. Her jaw was set in anger and determination. Tracey took her stance, looked at the window and with everything she had, let the rock fly. The battle stopped. The entire courtyard fell into a dead silence as everyone watched the flight of the rock. You could hear a pin drop. It was low; Tracey could see it was low. The rock struck the bottom part of the window sill and ricocheted up to the ceiling. Tracey dropped to her knees. She had failed.

Suddenly, Jason started bouncing up and down on the dragon yelling, "Yes, yes, yes, Tray, you did it."

The rock must have bounced off the ceiling and into the altar, thought Tracey.

There was a shriek from the balcony as the Evil One ran back into the castle. The evil army quickly withdrew, disappearing in all directions. The buzzards and hawks flew away. The window above the balcony started to glow softly. The dark clouds above the castle began to part and the sun shined through.

The window above the balcony now began to sparkle and glow brightly. The door to the castle opened and the Evil One staggered out. Now the whole courtyard was bathed in sparkling light. The Evil One stumbled and fell. King William and all those who had a spell on them began to drop. The sparkling light became so bright; everyone else had to cover their eyes.

When Tracey looked again, King William was rising to his feet, but————he was no longer a goat. King William looked handsome and wise. He looked like everything a King should look like. Sir George and Lady Jane were kissing. He was rugged and handsome and Lady Jane was beautiful.

King William limped over to his Queen. She lay face down on the ground, her dress no longer red but white. When King William turned her over, she was now the most beautiful woman Tracey had ever seen. The King cradled her head and kissed her softly. She was alive, but she wouldn't wake up.

All of a sudden, Tracey was being hugged. It was Jason. "I've got to get back to LB," he said; and then seeing the confused look on Tracey's face, he added, "LB is the dragon." Jill was still with Jason. She had become a cute little red haired girl, about Jason's age.

Tracey, regaining her senses, knelt next to Squire Josh. He was about 12 and very handsome. An arrow was lodged in his shoulder. Tracey tried to stop the bleeding. Squire Josh half opened his eyes, smiled and then grimaced with pain.

"Are you all right?" he asked Tracey.

"You're asking me if I'm all right," said Tracey, with tears in her eyes. "You're the one shot with an arrow." Tracey couldn't stop the bleeding. She screamed for help.

Many had fought and died that day to restore the most precious thing the human spirit can possess, freedom.

CHAPTER 17

▼

(THE FRIEND)

It had been two weeks since the battle. Tracey knelt, placed flowers on the grave and stood up. The castle grave yard was usually reserved only for high ranking royalty, but King William ordered that he be buried here. It was a fitting place for a brave young man.

Sir George was with Tracey. No longer the brave little rabbit that had hopped all the way across the kingdom with her, Sir George now stood tall and strong. He placed a comforting hand on Tracey's shoulder.

"He was a fine young man," said Sir George.

"During the battle, he saved the King's life, you know," said Tracey.

"Yes, I know," said Sir George softly.

It was near the end of the battle when Yuk made a mighty charge for King William. King William didn't see him coming. It was Tony, the brave little warrior, with an arrow in his leg, who limped in, driving his sword deep into Yuk. Yuk grabbed Tony and as he crushed the life out of him, Tony continued to drive the sword into Yuk, until the sword finally fell from his hand. Then Yuk fell, moved a little, and died with Tony.

The gravestone is beautiful," said Tracey.

The stone read, Tony—A Mighty Warrior—Slayer of Yuk.

"How is Squire Josh doing?" asked Sir George.

Tracey smiled, "He's doing really well. The doctor, or physician, as you call him, says he should be up and about tomorrow. Have you heard anything about Queen Genevive?"

"Nothing," said Sir George, "King William hardly ever leaves her side, day or night. She seems fine, but she won't wake up."

The weather was sunny, but had been turning chilly the last couple of days. Tracey buttoned up the collar on the coat that Lady Jane had found for her.

"Tray," it was Jason running toward the graveyard. He ran up to them, "Hey! Sir George, how'ya doin?" He had taught Sir George how to give him five, so they gave each other five. "They say there's a big storm coming in tonight," said Jason.

"Jay!" came a distant call. It was Jill, looking for Jason.

"I can't ever seem to get away from her," said Jason.

Tracey and Sir George laughed. "Jay, it looks like you have a little sweetie," laughed Tracey.

"Tray," said Jason, scrunching up his face, "give me a break. I mean, she's a really nice girl, but she doesn't know anything about the really important stuff. She never heard of baseball cards or comics or computers and doesn't even know how to fish."

Little red haired Jill spotted Jason, smiled and came running. Tracey and Sir George laughed.

When they got back to the castle, the villagers had brought a large pine tree from the forest and set it up in the great hall. The villagers and people of the castle were decorating it.

"Well, I'll be," said Sir George. "It's been many years since they've had a Friendship Tree and many more since The Friend has come leaving presents."

Tracey and Jason's eyes were wide with astonishment.

"We call it a Christmas Tree," said Tracey.

"And the one that comes bringing presents," added Jason, "we call Santa Clause."

Jill was excited. "Come on," she said excitedly, "let's go help decorate the tree."

Everyone was happy and sad at the same time. They hoped the tree and its decorations would help Queen Genevive, but it didn't. Toward evening, the wind got icy cold and the storm clouds rolled in. Before the villagers left, everyone knelt and prayed for Queen Genevive and all those who had died and were injured in the battle. Afterward, Sir George told Tracey, he couldn't remember the last time he saw everyone pray together. When the villagers left, everyone went to bed. As Tracey was on her way to her room, she passed King William's chambers. Two of his royal guards stood on each side of the great doors. The doors were open a crack. As Tracey walked by, she could see King William kneeling next to Queen Genevive's bed. He was praying.

The storm hit with a force during the night and then settled down. It was still very early in the morning, long before daybreak. Jason didn't know why he woke up so early, but he did. He ran over to the window and looked out. From the lights of the castle, he could see the courtyard was covered with snow and large white flakes still drifted down.

Jason ran down to the Great Hall. It was empty, lit only by the candles that burned high on the walls and the roaring fire in the fireplace at the end of the hall. Jason started to leave, when he noticed that around the tree were piled hundreds of presents that hadn't been there before. Something was moving in the shadows behind the tree. He cautiously crept over and peeked around the tree.

"Hello Jason," sang a voice, as he put the last of his presents under the tree. It was an old man, dressed in a gray suit and vest. He wore an old gray hat and white hair stuck out from under it. He had a smile you could barely see, behind a white fluffy beard "I told you that was a special rock," he smiled.

It was the old man from the beach. Jason just stood there, mouth open. It may have been the only time, since Jason learned to talk, that he was speechless.

"I dress a little differently here, than I do where you come from," smiled the old man. "Here," he chuckled, "they call me 'The Friend'. I am called many names and dress differently in many different places." The old man walked over to Jason and bent down. He became serious. "You see," he said, "there was almost no love left in this place. I couldn't come here any-more. The only things that could save them were the pure hearts and courage of two young people." Then he stood up and laughed, "And you and Tracey did a magnificent job. You see, there is only a little magic in the rock. The real magic is in the hearts of the people. When the rock is placed on the altar of light, its brightness only reflects the friendship and love that exists here." He gave a wonderful jolly laugh, "And it's never shone brighter than now."

"Well," he said laughing, "I have to go now." The old man walked over to the window and opened it. He turned and looked at Jason. "You wouldn't mind closing the window after me, would you? I hate using fireplaces with fires in them," he said laughing. "If you're not quick enough, you get singed," then he laughed again. "Oh, by the way, there's a very special present for you and Tracey, but don't peek." As he jiggled with laughter, he put his finger along side of his nose and up and out of the window he slipped.

Jason was still frozen and speechless as he heard the sound of sleigh bells fade away. Finally he went over to the window, looked out and closed it.

Jason ran into Tracey's room and jumped on her big canopy bed. "Tray—Tray," he said excitedly, as he shook her, "wake up."

Tracey sat up, still half asleep. "Jason, it's not even light out. What now?"

"Tray," he said, still very excited, "the old man on the beach was Santa Clause, or at least he's like our Santa Claus. I've always wondered how he knew our names that day on the beach, and now I just saw him downstairs by the tree."

Tracey flopped back on her pillow and closed her eyes. "Jason," she said, a little irritated, "you're getting weird again. It's only a dream. Now go back to bed." Tracey turned over on her side to go back to sleep.

"But Tray," said Jason, pleadingly.

"Jason," said Tracey loudly, "go back to bed."

Jason sulked back to his room. Hombre was lying on the bed. Jason laid down next to Hombre. "I know that they're never going to believe me," Jason said to Hombre. Jason was sure he wouldn't be able to go back to sleep. In ten minutes, he was sleeping soundly.

CHAPTER 18

▼

(THE MAGIC RETURNS)

"Jason, wake up." It was Tracey, shaking him. Jason sat up in bed and rubbed his eyes. A ray of sunlight stole through the drapes covering his windows and lit up a spot on the floor.

"Look, Jay," said Tracey excitedly, as she pulled back the drapes. The bright sunlight blinded Jason's sleepy eyes for a moment. Jason scrunched up his face and squinted.

"Isn't it beautiful?" said Tracey, looking out the window, into the courtyard.

Jason climbed out of bed and walked over to the window, still squinting his eyes in the bright light.

Outside, the courtyard was like a fairyland. The storm from last night had passed, leaving the whole area covered in a blanket of pure white snow. Icicles hung everywhere and sparkled in the early morning sun. There wasn't a cloud to be seen anywhere in the rich blue sky.

"Come on," said Tracey, still excited, "hurry up and get dressed. There's something going on downstairs."

As Tracey and Jason descended the stairway, their eyes were wide at the scene before them. The villagers and the people of the castle were all in the Great Hall, smiling, hugging and laughing softly. When Tracey saw the piles of presents around the tree, she knew that Jason hadn't been dreaming.

Tracey and Jason moved through the crowd. They were being hugged and thanked by so many people they didn't even know, but who knew them. It didn't take long for little red-headed Jill to find Jason and the three of them went over to talk to Sir George and Lady Jane.

Tracey looked around the crowd. "King William must still be with Queen Genevive," she said, still looking.

"Yes," said Lady Jane, "they're about the only ones not here. We were so hoping she would be better."

"How is your dragon, LB doing?" Sir George asked Jason.

LB had been seriously wounded in the battle and was recovering in her own wing of the castle.

"She's almost better," answered Jason. "Jill and I are going to see her later. She's going to have to stay here in the castle until the weather warms up. She'd never be able to make it back to the warm swamp."

Sir George and Lady Jane started grinning at Tracey.

Tracey smiled and looked at them. They kept grinning at her. "What?" she said grinning back. "Well——what?" she said laughing and shrugging her shoulders. Tracey felt a tap on her shoulder. As she turned around, someone kissed her on the cheek. Squire Josh was standing there grinning, one arm in a sling and the other holding some mistletoe over Tracey's head.

Tracey blushed, "Josh, you're up." Tracey gave him a quick hug, being careful of his wounded shoulder.

"Jason," said Squire Josh. "Would you like to borrow my mistletoe?"

Jill was smiling and blushing.

"Very funny Josh," blushed Jason as everyone else laughed. "You know, Josh," said Jason, "I think I liked you better when you were a dog. In fact in some ways, you still are a dog." This time everybody laughed, including Jason.

The buzz of excitement in the room completely stopped. It was so quiet; you could hear a pin drop. Everyone in the Great Hall was staring at the top of the staircase. There, at the top of the staircase, stood King William and next to him, stood the beautiful and smiling Queen Genevive.

As King William and Queen Genevive started down the stairs, the Great Hall exploded with cheers and applause. People were laughing and wiping tears of joy from their eyes. Many fell to their knees and gave thanks. This day of Friendship would truly be a day to remember. The true magic had returned. It was no longer the Land of Cigam; it was once again Magic Land.

The rest of the day would be filled with laughter and merriment, dancing and feasting. Tracey and Jason met and visited with Queen Genevive. She was so beautiful and charming, thought Tracey. When she smiled, which she did often, everything around her seemed to light up. King William had told her about their journey and how they never would have made it without Tracey and Jason. Queen Genevive thanked them and hugged them both. Tracey had never seen King William so happy.

Later, Jason and Jill ran off to check on LB. They had gathered several things from the feast that they thought a dragon might like. Tracey and Josh sat laughing and talking. They talked about their journey and how King William had told Josh he would almost certainly be a Knight like Sir George when he got older. The music and laughter continued around them. Tracey kept glancing at King William and Queen Genevive, thinking how happy they looked. Even though Tracey sat in the middle of so many happy people and loved visiting with Josh, she felt a little sad and lonely. She missed her family.

It was early evening before they started opening the presents. One by one, the presents were slowly handed out by Queen Genevive, so that everyone could savor this wonderful day as long as possible. With all the people of the castle and the villagers it seemed to Tracey and Jason like it would take forever. What was the special present that had been left for them? Each time Queen Genevive picked up a present and read the name, Tracey and Jason hoped it was theirs and each time, the anticipation grew. The huge pile of presents gradually disappeared, until, buried at the bottom, one last present remained. It was a large box marked for Tracey and Jason. It was moved to the center of the Great Hall so everyone could see. There was a bow at the top and a string attached. On the string was a little sign that read 'pull'. Tracey and Jason pulled the string together and the box fell open. There, just like the day that they had built it, sat the little cardboard airplane.

CHAPTER 19

▼

(HOME)

The day before had been a day that Tracey would never forget. When she finally went to bed, she was exhausted from so much happiness. When she woke in the morning, she felt totally refreshed and ready for a very special day.

The Royal Tailor had made both of them clothes exactly like the old tattered clothes they had worn on their journey. Tracey and Jason had bathed, dressed and met at the end of the long hallway leading to the stairs into the Great Hall. When Tracey saw Jason, she hardly recognized him in his new clothes, face clean and hair combed.

"Jay, you look nice," Tracey smiled. "You sure got grubby looking when we were on our journey."

"It didn't bother me," said Jason, as he ruffled his newly combed hair.

They started off down the long wide hallway toward the Great Hall. An Honor guard stood smiling, at attention, up and down both sides of the hallway.

"I can't believe we're finally going home," said Tracey. "It's going to be so good to see Mom and Dad again."

"Yeah," said Jason, "do you think they're going to be really mad?"

"I'm hoping they'll be too happy to see us to be too angry," smiled Tracey.

"I wish we could take LB back with us," said Jason.

"Right," said Tracey, "and where are you going to keep a dragon? She wouldn't even fit in the house, let alone your room."

"I guess you're right," said Jason dejectedly. "But it would be nice. I could take her to school for Show and Tell." Smiling, he added, "LB is going to live in the castle you know. At least she won't be lonely anymore."

"You know," Tracey said, with a puzzled look on her face, "I've been meaning to ask you, how did LB get her name."

"I gave it to her," smiled Jason. "She didn't have a name, so I named her."

"Well, why LB?" asked Tracey. "What does it mean?"

"It's just a name, It doesn't mean anything," said Jason, shaking his head.

"Jason," said Tracey, squinting at him, a hint of anger in her voice, "what does LB mean?"

They walked a little further and Jason didn't answer. Tracey stopped, put her hands on her hips and glared at Jason. "Jason, you're going to tell me before we go another step."

Jason stopped and turned. "Tray," he said sheepishly, "I named her before I knew how nice she was."

"All right," said Tracey, "what's the L stand for?"

Jason rolled his eyes up, "Lizard."

"Jason," Tracey said angrily, "you named her lizard? She's a dragon, not a lizard."

"Tray, that's all dragons are, — big lizards," argued Jason.

"OK," said Tracey, trying to control her anger, "what's the B stand for?"

"Breath," said Jason, knowing she would get it out of him anyway. "Tray, I feel bad about giving her that name, but it's done. Besides, how would you like her to breathe on you? You'd look like an over-done pop tart. If there's anyone in the whole world that needs a truck load of breath mints more than she does, I sure don't want to meet them."

"Jason, I don't believe this," Tracey said, her face turning red from anger, "you named her Lizard Breath? You know sometimes you can be so cruel. Since the day we got here, you've insulted everyone," said Tracey. "You called King William, Billy Goat."

"Well, he was," said Jason.

"You whacked off the end of King William's tail at the bridge and later cut another big chunk out of it when we were fighting the scorpions," said Tracey.

"That was to save our lives," argued Jason.

"You wet on Sir George," said Tracey.

"That was an accident, I didn't see him," chuckled Jason, "and besides the wind came up."

"Jason, I don't remember any wind that day," said Tracey, "and later on you thumped Sir George on the head with your club."

"I might have saved his life," said Jason, "a scorpion was going to get him."

Then during the battle," said Tracey, "You hit King William in the foot with Steve, the Rock. King William is still limping a little bit."

"Tracey are you sure you couldn't have caught that rock?" asked Jason.

"That rock was way over my head Jason," said Tracey, "and you know it."

And down the hall they went, arguing back and forth.

As Tracey and Jason came down the stairway to the Great Hall, the room erupted with cheers and applause. Everyone had crowded into the Great Hall to say good-bye. The Hall was filled with well-wishers; even LB had recovered enough to come. There was about a ten foot space around LB. It seemed that every time she got a little emotional, she would snort out a little fire. No one was taking any chances; they didn't want to get their hair singed.

There was also a wide pathway leading to the far side of the Hall, where King William and Queen Genevive were seated on the throne. King William had removed the bandage from his foot, where Jason had hit him with the rock. Standing next to them were Sir George and Lady Jane. The bruise on Sir George's forehead, where Jason had whacked him with his club, was almost completely gone and only a small reddish dot remained.

Everyone, especially King William and Queen Genevive were dressed very formally and looked magnificent.

When Tracey and Jason reached the throne, King William held up his hand and the Great Hall fell into silence.

"Tracey and Jason," said King William, "we are indebted to you for coming to our land and helping us to restore our Kingdom. We couldn't have done it without you. We had lost our Kingdom because of our own selfishness. We had somehow forgotten love, friendship, humility, caring and the true giving of ourselves for others in need. We had lost all the finest qualities that make us human beings. We know now that the greatest magic in the rock Jason named Steve, is that it reflects those qualities in its brightness. The more love and friendship, the brighter it glows. For years, we hadn't noticed that each year it got dimmer and dimmer. We had become so selfish, so self-centered and so uncaring toward our fellow human beings that at last, it hardly glowed at all. This allowed the evil seeds that always exist to take hold and grow. And as the evil grew, we either didn't notice or didn't care, until it was too late. We know that evil will always exist, but as long as we love and care about each other and stand up for what is right, it will never be more than a seed. We have lost many friends and loved ones to learn this bitter lesson. It is a lesson we shall never forget. I have also learned from you, Tracey and Jason, that whether you are a servant or a King, we are all of equal value. Tracey and Jason, we owe you everything."

The Great Hall burst out with cheers and applause that lasted for several minutes. King William had Tracey and Jason come up and stand beside the throne next to him and Queen Genevive. Many people were laughing and hugging and crying. Twice, LB almost burned someone as her great dragon tears splashed on the floor and she accidentally snorted out fire. Finally, when things calmed down, King William again held up his hand and the Great Hall fell into silence.

"At this time, I would also like to honor our dragon, LB, for her great contribution to our success. During the battle, she fearlessly risked her own life, sustaining serious wounds." The King looked at Jason and in a low voice asked, "Does she have another name besides LB?"

Jason started to say something, but Tracey interrupted him. She was squinting at him again, so he knew to shut up.

"Your Majesty," said Tracey, "my brother is not very good at spelling. The initials should have been EB, short for Elizzardbreath," then Tracey stuttered, "I—-I mean Elizabeth." Out of the corner of her eye, Tracey saw Jason snickering.

King William sat for a moment. "Elizabeth," he said thoughtfully, "that's a marvelous name. But, it's up to our dragon. Then, in a loud voice, "What say you dragon? Would you like to be known by Elizabeth?"

LB smiled, blushed, nodded her head up and down and thumped her tail on the ground.

"So be it" said King William. "Henceforth, you shall be known as Lady Elizabeth, Dragon of the Kingdom and Royal Fire Starter."

At this point, a servant, dressed in what appeared to be some sort of fire-proof suit, carefully approached LB. He carried a large ribbon, on which hung an official medallion. LB lowered her head so the servant could put it around her neck. The servant got out of the way just in time, almost getting singed. The Great Hall was again filled with cheers and applause.

While the cheering was going on, King William leaned toward Jason. "Does the dragon talk at all?" asked King William.

"Yes," answered Jason, "but it's the eggs."

"What eggs?" asked King William, a little confused.

"Her husband was killed by the Evil One about two years ago," said Jason.

"Oh! I had no idea," said King William, surprised at the knowledge.

"It seems," continued Jason, "that it takes dragons a little over two years for their eggs to develop, so, as soon as she lays her eggs next month, she'll be talking up a storm again."

King William looked visibly shaken. "How many eggs will she lay?" he asked.

Jason smiled, "Only about three or four," he replied.

"You mean," said King William, growing paler by the minute, "that we're going to have three or four little fire starters running around the castle?"

Jason, smiling broadly, shook his head up and down.

"Good grief!" said King William, slumping back on his throne. "We're going to have to organize a fire brigade to follow them around." Then as if he were thinking out loud, "I wonder if she would mind going back to the swamp, just until they're fire-broken?"

As the cheering and applause subsided, King William snapped back to reality and composed himself. However, he still looked a little pale.

"Now." said King William, very solemnly, "the reason we have gathered here today, is to say good-bye to Tracey and Jason." King William clapped his hands three times and two Knights came into the Great Hall, carrying the little cardboard airplane. Riding in the front and back seats, all cleaned up and brushed, were L'il Lucas, the little brown bear and Hombre, the little brown dog. Tracey and Jason walked around the plane, looking at it.

Tracey looked at Jason, "It seems so long ago." She picked up L'il Lucas, looked at him and tucked him under her arm. Tracey walked over and hugged and kissed Queen Genevive, King William, Lady Jane and Sir George. Jason tried to shake hands with all of them, but Queen Genevive and Lady Jane hugged and kissed him anyway. He didn't protest too much.

Tracey looked around the crowd, but didn't see Josh. Jason turned and waived at LB and everyone backed up another ten feet and for good reason. The dragon snorted out a big flame and a huge tear splashed on the stone floor.

Jason walked over to the pedestal where 'Steve', the Rock, sat glowing more brightly than anyone could remember. He picked Steve up and walked back to the plane. Jason started to get in front.

"No you don't," said Tracey, "this time I'm riding in front."

Jason was in no mood to argue, besides, she was squinting at him again. "OK," said Jason, "it's all yours." Jason climbed in back with Hombre and Tracey got in front with L'il Lucas. Tracey turned half way around and Jason handed her Steve. She looked at Jason, "Jay, you've got a tear in your eye."

"I do not," he said quietly, "It's only a piece of dirt."

Suddenly, Josh came out of the crowd, out of breath. He ran up to Tracey, holding something behind his back, with his good arm. Josh smiled, "This is for you Tracey." From behind his back, he handed her a beautiful red rose.

"Thank you Josh," said Tracey blushing.

"I almost didn't make it," he said, still out of breath. "Since the weather changed, it's the last one in the green house. The keeper wasn't going to let me have it, until I told him it was for you." He quickly bent down and kissed Tracey on the cheek. "I'll miss you," he said and backed away waving. Tracey's blush was almost as red as the rose Josh gave her.

Jason rolled his eyes back and shook his head. "Tray," he said, "couldn't we have left without all that mushy stuff?"

As Tracey turned around to tell him to shut up, Jill came running out of the crowd. By the time Jason saw her out of the corner of his eye, it was too late. As he slumped down in the back seat, Jill planted a big kiss on his cheek and ran back into the crowd.

The Great Hall burst into roars of laughter as Jason's blush almost matched Tracey's. King William almost fell off his throne, he was laughing so hard.

"Tray," said Jason, still blushing, "it's definitely time to go."

"Are you sure," said Tracey giggling, "Don't you want one more kiss from your sweetie?"

Jason slumped down in the back seat, shaking his head back and forth and rolling his eyes up, "Give me a break."

Tracey, still laughing, put Steve in the little shoe box on the front of the plane. The plane had been placed so that the morning sun would shine on it. People in the Great Hall were waving, wiping tears and some were still laughing. LB was just trying not to burn anybody.

It didn't take long before the sparkles started to swirl around the plane. Steve grew brighter and brighter and then there was a flash. Tracey and Jason blinked, trying to focus their eyes.

"Are you gremlins going to play in here all day? You should be outside. It's a beautiful day."

Tracey and Jason looked up stunned. "Dad," they both said at the same time.

Another head popped in the doorway. "We're going to eat lunch in about five minutes, so get washed up."

"Mom," they both said surprised, sitting with their eyes wide, mouths open;

"Are you guys feeling all right?" Mom said, with a worried look on her face.

"Yeah," answered Tracey.

"Yeah," answered Jason, his eyes still wide, mouths still open.

Mom and Dad looked at each other, shrugged and left.

The next day, Tracey and Jason talked Mom and Dad into taking them to the ocean for a picnic. The beach they went to was often deserted. Tracey and Jason sat Indian style on a large black rock near the water. Lucas and Hombre were tucked safely in their laps. They sat for a long time, not saying a word, watching the waves rolling in. There was a morning haze in the air, but the sun would soon burn that off.

"Do you think we should tell Mom and Dad what happened?" said Jason.

"I don't think so," said Tracey, "I heard Mom talking to Dad this morning and they already think we're acting weird. If we told them what happened, they'd probably take us to a doctor or something."

"Yeah," said Jason, "I guess you're right."

"Jay," said Tracey, "I think it's time to send Steve back home now."

Jason reached in his pocket and took Steve out.

"Can I hold him for a minute?" asked Tracey. She cupped her hands and held Steve gently. "Good-bye and thank you," she whispered. "If you could talk, I'd have you say hello to Josh." Steve glowed brightly and dimmed again.

Jason said good-bye to Steve. He carried him over and put him on the ground, on the other side of the big rock that they were sitting on, along with the red rose that Josh had given Tracey.

Tracey and Jason sat and watched. In a short time, the sparkles began to form around Steve. There was a flash and he was gone, along with the rose. They sat quietly for a little while; then they climbed down off the rock they had been sitting on. They started back down the beach to where Mom and Dad had spread some blankets.

"Do you think they will ever send Steve back to get us?" asked Jason.

"Get serious," chuckled Tracey. "After what you did to those people, they'd have to be pretty desperate. Although, it would be nice to see Josh again sometime and you have to admit," said Tracey smiling, "Jill was pretty cute."

Jason blushed a little. Then he said, "Well, maybe Jill was a little cute," and quickly added, "but just a little and that's all."

They walked on the hard wet part of the sand, just above where the waves were coming in. The sea gulls flew in and out and the ocean breeze felt nice.

"Tray," said Jason, "do you really think it was Santa Clause who showed me where to find Steve?"

"I don't know," said Tracey, "he was somebody. What do you think?"

TRACEY—JASON," it was Mom walking down the beach toward them.

Jason yelled, "I'll race you," and he took off down the beach toward Mom. Tracey kept walking and when she got to Mom and Jason, Mom put an arm around their shoulders and off down the beach they went. Jason hopping and swinging Hombre. Tracey, with l'il Lucas under her arm, thinking how nice it was to be home and wondering what kind of a mess Jason was going to get her into next.

The End of the Beginning

Tracey moved about the kitchen while helping Mom clean-up after dinner. Through an open window, a thud could be heard every few seconds as a baseball hit a glove. Dad and Jason were outside playing catch. Tracy stopped and stared out the window at them. Jason had taken the whole adventure in stride as if nothing had ever happened. Tracey felt uneasiness within her as if something was not quite right. Suddenly an arm went around Tracey's shoulders and Tracey looked up. Mom was standing next to her watching Dad and Jason. Mom looked down at Tracey and smiled.

"Did you have a good summer Tray?"

"Yah Mom," Tracey smiled.

Mom turned facing Tracey, pulling her close and giving her a hug.

"It seems hard to believe," said mom as she pulled away. "You're eleven years old now and getting ready to start sixth grade in two days. The summer has swept by so fast and you seem to have grown up so much these last three months. You should be playing outside."

"I just don't feel like it Mom. I just want to be in here with you," answered Tracey.

"You seem a little troubled" said Mom. "Is there anything you want to talk about?"

"No," answered Tracey—"nothing."

Mom reached out and put a hand on each of Tracey's shoulders and looked her in the eyes while smiling softly. "Are you sure?"

"Yes," answered Tracey. "I'm sure." Tracey wanted to tell mom about everything; but, something held her back. Why couldn't she just say what happened? Mom would probably think she was crazy and would never understand. Besides, it was over now and best forgotten.

Mom stood for a moment searching Tracey's eyes. Mom smiled and gave Tracey another hug.

"It's just your mom," Mom said. "I'm probably just imagining things."

What Tracey couldn't see was Mom's smile disappearing and turning into a look of concern as she continued hugging Tracey?

Tracey was alone in a small boat on the ocean. The little boat would rise and fall with the swells as the wind whipped across her face. Each time the swells got higher as Tracey held on as hard as she could. Tracey closed her eyes as the little boat lurched about. The motion stopped.

When Tracey opened her eyes, she was on a mountainside. She was desperately looking for something; but, she didn't know what. Tracey could feel something was after her—something menacing and powerful. Time was running out. Her heart was pounding. TIME WAS RUNNING OUT.... .

Tracey quickly sat up in bed—eyes wide and heart pounding. She was drenched in sweat. The dream had awakened something within her. What was going on? Why didn't she tell Mom?

Tracey got out of bed to get a drink of water in the bathroom. It was late. The house was very quiet as she walked down the hall. She heard a muffled voice coming from down stairs. Tracey crept softly to about halfway down the stairs and stopped. The voice was her mothers. Tracey strained to hear. "Yes," her mother said. "I know it's not time; but, she seems to have all the signs." .... "I know it's two or three generations away; but, I think it's happening." .... "I hope we still have time. I'll keep an eye on her. Will you tell the others?" .... "I love you Grandma. Goodbye."

Tracey quickly made her way back to her bedroom. Tracey sat on the edge of her bed for a long time. It seems that she has been drawn into something she has no control over. What did mom mean? When she said, "She shows all the signs."—Signs of what? How is Jason involved in all of this? What do the dreams mean? Tracey finally laid down and went to sleep.

978-0-595-46947-5
0-595-46947-7

Printed in the United States
96249LV00001B/76-123/A